Some Effing Advice

Tasmia Nishat

1

"Habs beat Flames 4-2. The Flames were leading up until the last period, and then—"

"Out of *nowhere*, the Habs got two goals in!"

"Flames are still winning overall, so we'll see with the next two games, eh? It's gonna be a nail-biter, alright…"

Shelia had no doubt it was going to be a nail-biter, and that she would get to hear exclusively about every single nail-biting detail for the next few weeks, whether she gave a shit about them or not. *You'd think after all of my years working in semi-bro environments, I'd adapt by watching a freaking hockey game.*

Despite the draw of sporty camaraderie, she never did, and thus, she found herself zoning out during many a lunch with her colleagues, which included people from different departments. There was Mark, offender #1 for hockey and beer enthusiasm. There was the obscenely affable Jeremiah, whose presence Shelia appreciated as it prevented her from being the minority in IT. There was Lily, Anthony, James, Connor, whatsherface: a whole host of people who were nice enough but in the end, were the kind of friendships that happened because of their sheer proximity to each other. *Friendships of convenience,* Shelia thought: after all, having somebody, even if you didn't quite relate to them, was better than having nobody.

After lunch, Shelia continued working on uninspired coding projects, made bearable by intermittently playing *Monkey Quest*. She maniacally fought off a green bouncy blob, pressing buttons in a convoluted manner. The blob triumphed over the monkey in a single, well-executed body slam.

"Goddamnit," Shelia said, slumping away from the screen and into her seat.

"Still playing Monkey Quest, I see," someone chuckled behind her, amused. It was no secret at the office that Shelia had a love-hate relationship with Monkey Quest.

The chuckler pulled her light brown hair away from her face, which was almost the same shade as her skin tone. This move highlighted her manicured fingers, sharp and bold like her eyebrows.

The woman settled into Shelia's cubicle. "You know that book I recommended to you a while back? Apparently they're gonna make a movie out of it," she said idly. She looked at Shelia earnestly. "You have to read it, Shelia. It will awaken your soul."

It was Olivia, and nary a day went by when she didn't mention the word 'soul'. This was ironic given Olivia, like Shelia, was a fellow cog in the nine to five machine. On corporate servitude, she would say: "Okay, look, I think the whole 'cubicle cog' thing is a dangerous stereotype. All work can be fulfilling, as long as it's done with *intention*."

She was racially ambiguous and gorgeous, and Sheila thought she ought to be a model instead of a fellow coworker-slave. Though, with her average pear-shaped body type, she could probably only do catalogues. A fact that made Shelia feel a bit better.

"Wow. I didn't realize the fact that my soul was asleep was so obvious."

She glanced at the clock—*time to get the fuck out of here.* She stretched her arms and packed up, chattering with her coworkers on the way out.

"Did you see the boss' new toupee?"

"Yeah. It suits him!"

They all chuckled, and parted ways. A sense of quiet emptiness pervaded her being on her walk home, as it occasionally did. The clap of her step hitting the concrete rang cold, and the faces of the strangers she passed by seemed like walls. Did they feel like this too, or were they bluffing like she was?

She imagined herself in the future, about 12 minutes from now. What would she do when she got home, exactly? She would walk up the creaky, metal stair case. Shimmy her keys into the door, plop onto her suede couch; the dust from the plop would fly up in a slow, spiralling dance, without her knowledge. And then: working on that boring-ass project until eight, emails, T.V.

How did she end up like this?

She desperately wished to prolong what felt like the inevitable return to her slow-burning doom. She impulsively took a right turn instead of going straight, deciding to ignore all of her pending work for now.

The burst of unfamiliarity emboldened her. Left for three blocks, right for five, and then another right: frenzied at first, but in time, slow and taking in the new sights. One sight in particular caught her eye, of a traditional red-and-blue lit 'open' sign. The door was reminiscent of a chocolate bar with its three-by-three paneling, its white paint job peeling. The green and gold sign—'Yoyo's Books'—was also worn.

Trance-like, Shelia decided to come in. Something jangled behind her. Shelia looked up, startled, hoping to identify the offending item. It was: a single, tiny bell.

"My my, you startle easy," said an old-womanly voice from behind the counter. It belonged to a Filipino woman who lowered her glasses to peer at her critically. Or was she Aboriginal? Frankly, Shelia was surprised it wasn't a white younger person behind the counter. Not that she was racist. Seriously.

Shelia didn't know how to respond to that, so she smiled a non-smile. The woman gave her a bemused look and went back to whatever the shit she was doing before.

The place was faded, but colourful. Red shelves, yellow rugs, and assorted knick-knacks abound, such as that rubber chicken holding a "Nothing is certain but death and taxes" sign in the corner. And there was a weird smell: the smell of books? *Damn, it's been a while.*

Shelia dutifully thumbed through a book or two, but she didn't know what she was doing in the cramped place. After what she felt was a sufficient amount of pretend-browsing, Shelia left. A tinkling noise marked her departure.

"Later," the cashier said gruffly.

When she reached her apartment, she was struck with the urge to read a big, consuming, novel. A search of her place yielded nothing suitable. She sighed, and worked on a project into the night.

She hadn't meant to return to Yoyo's books, but she did just that two weeks later. In all that time she had gone wandering exactly once, and she had discovered a surprisingly cheap phở place. She'd meant to do it more, but, *you know, I'm busy with work.*

It was a Thursday. The anticipation of Friday had Shelia in a lighter mood, so she went exploring. By chance, she was in the vicinity of Yoyo's Books once again.

She was going to pass it by, but she noticed something familiar in the window: a book called 'A Practical Guide to Life'. Where had she heard of it before? *Hmm… Oh, yes, Olivia.* Was Shelia really going to buy a book recommended from Olivia? Shelia secretly (or not-so-secretly) thought all of her go-go positive vibes were bullshit, but she had to admit, bitch had it going on. Minus the soul-sucking job. But Olivia, amazingly, didn't seem to mind that either. Maybe this book would reveal Olivia's secret to not hating your life.

"Hello!" Shelia called out brightly. The cashier was the same person from two weeks ago. This time, Shelia was not going to be an awkward fuck.

"Hi. What can I do ya for," the cashier said monotonously. Unconsciously, Shelia scrutinized her face, trying to figure out—

"What the heck are you staring at, kid?" inquired the cashier.

"Um. Nothing," She said quickly. *Probably Aboriginal*, Shelia decided privately. "I'd like to buy this," she said, sliding over 'A Practical Guide to Life'.
The cashier rang the book up, whistling. As she was doing this, Shelia noticed some water stains on it.

"Wait, is this book used?"

"Yup. Adds more character. And is easier on the wallet," she winked.
Used wasn't Shelia's thing, but she decided to forgo her preferences for now. She handed Shelia 'A Practical Guide to Life' and some change without another word, and Shelia headed towards the door. But before leaving, Shelia turned around abruptly. "Um. By the way, are you... Yoyo?"
The cashier smiled. "Indeed I am."

"Ah. Nice establishment," she murmured as she turned to leave.

Olivia peeked her head over her cubicle wall. Her expression was jubilant. "Shelia, guess what?" she grinned. *What could it be? A new juicing cleanse that I've just *got* to try? Positive-thinking mantras? Achievement of enlightenment?*

"Mhm?" Shelia said patiently.

"I got promoted," she said, stage-whispering the last word. She blinked. Shelia was surprised: she thought she'd land the promotion that was open to employees of all branches. Yes, Shelia hated her job, but she thought she was still pretty good at it. *Good enough for a promotion, at least.* But apparently not.

Shelia exerted all her willpower to not grimace at the news. *Have a pleasant expression, have a pleasant expression, have a pleasant expression…*

"Wow. That's fantastic. Congrats," she said, with what she hoped was some cheer.

"They'll announce it officially at the meeting, but for now, you're the first to know!" Olivia ducked and commenced packing up her belongings, presumably to move them to her new, fancy corner office.

The noise from Olivia's bustle in the next cubicle made Shelia feel tight. It was the sound of advancement, and leaving schmoops like Shelia in the dust.

"I bought that book you recommended," Shelia called out abruptly. "A Practical Guide to Life."

Olivia poked her head up to raise her eyebrows at Shelia.

"What?" Shelia asked.

Olivia looked amused. "I'm just happy that you actually took my recommendation. What do you think of it so far?"

"Well… I haven't actually read it," she said sheepishly.

"Let me know when you do. It's life-changing."

"I'll be sure to do that." Shelia said. Olivia returned to what she was doing.

A little later, Olivia passed by the entrance of Shelia's cubicle, her arms full with the last of her things. "Don't worry about things changing between us. I'm not going to let hierarchal structures get in the way of our friendship," Olivia assured. Sheila nodded, and tried for a smile. *Our friendship…* Shelia wondered, as Olivia left her cubicle for good: what was the nature of their friendship, anyway?

~

Shelia had started working at Womcroft Solutions a month after Olivia had. (In a couple months, Shelia would forget the real name of the company and replace it with Cogville in her head.)

"Hi! I'm Olivia," The impressive-looking woman said warmly, while extending her hand.

Huh. I wonder what race she is? Shelia shook it with her trademark jellyfish style. "Shelia."

"Sheel-a or Sheel-yuh?"

8

"Sheel-yuh."

Olivia had immediately tasked herself with imparting the knowledge she had gained in one month's time to Shelia.

"Okay, so we all know about the bathrooms on the main floor. They're what you'd expect a bathroom in this place to be. Not good, not bad. But, if you take a left," she said as she made the said left, "and go down these stairs, there's this bathroom that nobody uses. It's great. It's almost meditative." Shelia paced the apparently mystical bathroom. It was white; sterile. One could definitely hear their own thoughts. Shelia was not particularly interested in listening to her thoughts.

"Do you actually… meditate in here?" Shelia asked, skeptical.

"No. But maybe I should," she mused.

Shelia placed her belongings in her new cubicle, christening it as her own. The place where she would henceforth spend forty hours a week, 261 days a year. She was relieved to have found a stable, well-paying job.

She surveyed her surroundings, feeling comfortable.

"Hey, we're cubbie buddies!" Olivia exclaimed, in what would be the first of many times she would pop her head over the cubicle wall to converse with Shelia.

Shelia glanced up at Olivia. "Oh, yeah, ha ha…" she said, startled.

"Oh, I didn't mean to scare you," Olivia said, amused. "So, listen, it's almost lunch. I know it's kind of random, but… do you want to get outta here and check out the fish store with me?" she asked.

"The... fish store?" Shelia blinked.

"Yeah. The fish are so beautiful. They're all sorts of vibrant colours. I find it so relaxing, looking at them swimming along."

Shelia didn't know what to make of this offer. "Thanks," she said politely, "but I should probably get more settled first."

"Alright. Next time!" Olivia said, her head disappearing within the confines of the cubicle wall once again. There never was a next time.

Despite both of them being in their mid-to-late twenties, Olivia had maintained the quirkiness that was acceptable for a goddamn teenager. To Shelia, she was a novel creature. But too alien: unsafe to get close to.

~

Ten minutes later, back in the present, Olivia passed by Shelia's cubicle again. "Hey, did you see that cat video I sent you?" Olivia asked.

Sheila was a little taken aback. She was used to just seeing Olivia's head above the cubicle wall. The full-length version of her would take some getting used to.

"Uh, no, I didn't," Shelia replied. She was still digesting the news of Olivia's promotion. "I'll look at it now," she said cheerily. She hoped internet cats would distract her from wallowing in envy.

Finally, the rest of the colleague chums had heard the news. They had finished their meeting and were heading out.

"Congrats on the promotion Olivs!" boomed Mark, clapping her on the shoulder.

"Thanks," Olivia beamed.

"We're celebrating with drinks," he declared.

"Yes, absolutely," Shelia agreed. She needed to escape from her brain. She needed to get really, really drunk.

"Let's not go to Millers. Let's check out that new bar that opened on fifth," Jeremiah said.

"What? Why? We always go to Millers!" Shelia protested.

"Exactly. We need to shake things up in honour of the new world order our girl Olivia is about to establish," he said.

"Ha! New World Order. I love it," Olivia said.

"That's actually literally the perfect way to describe Olivia," Lily chimed in.

Shelia fought to suppress a groan. *Ugh. What is with this circle jerk idol worship? With all other topics, these guys are dull as hell but when it comes to Olivia, it's like they come to life.*

The gang of coworkers passed by the new(ish) recruit known to Shelia as whatsherface, who was in the midst of putting on her coat.

"Hey," Olivia interrupted. "Elizabeth right?"

She nodded.

"You should come join us for a drink!" Olivia said, smiling. Elizabeth looked surprised at first, and then smiled back. "Sure. That might be fun," she said.

"This is sort of in a sketchy neighbourhood," Shelia remarked, as they were walking towards the bar.

"I concur," Lily said, looking around her.

"It's not that bad. It just gets a bad rap," Jeremiah said, as the group walked in.

"You know what? I think it has character. And it's great that this bar opened up here. New businesses are the key to revitalizing a neighbourhood," Olivia said, pushing through throngs of people; mostly a younger crowd. The lights were dim, and the atmosphere was pleasantly abuzz with social interaction.

"I think that's called gentrification," Jeremiah pointed out.

"In many cases, yes—but I think it's possible to balance revitalization without pushing out long-time residents, if you have proper controls put in place," Olivia said.

"Ever the master of the balancing act," Lily said. "Olivia for Prime Minister next election!" she shouted, laughing.

"Ha, I'm flattered! I'm not sure I'm into the schmoozy world of politics, though."
Shelia blurted, "That's surprising. I mean, our job is basically kissing ass all day. But now, Olivia, you get to kiss slightly less of it!"

The group was silent. The background noise of the bar filled in the silence, making it slightly less awkward. *Shit, I went too far,* Shelia thought nervously. She could usually keep such thoughts to herself. Why did she have to blurt it out now? Then, Jeremiah chuckled, to Shelia's relief. "Shelia, you've got it all wrong. Olivia is above us mere mortals," he said with a flourish, "and can get by without kissing ass!"

They all laughed. Shelia did too, happy at the broken silence.

"I'm so disheartened that you guys feel like that, you know? I don't think it has to be that way." Olivia said.

"Well, that gives me hope," Elizabeth said, who had been quiet up until that point.

"Yeah. Maybe the culture will change by the time you get settled in here, Liz," Mark said sardonically. He had a penchant for nicknaming people prematurely.

They all took their seats. "Shot of vodka, please," Shelia called out.

"Scotch," said Olivia. Olivia looked exasperated. "Okay, but remember, you guys are part of the culture. If you want it to change, you have to change it yourselves!"

As everyone else ordered their drinks, Mark said, "Oh really? That's a little naïve. Don't you think that there are counteracting forces from above preventing that from happening?"

Shelia was surprised. Shelia thought that Mark was nothing more than a dudebro who only cared about sports, but looked like dudebro had some teeth.

Jeremiah said, "Forces or no forces, do you think sitting on our butts and moping about our bosses is going to do anything? I'm with Olivia."

Mark said nothing and sipped his drink stoically. Elizabeth looked down, visibly unsure of what to do with herself, and Lily looked between Jeremiah and Mark nervously.

Shelia, conversely, was excited by the development. She didn't relish conflict, per se, (or did she? Nah, she probably didn't), but this real-talk was a refreshing change of pace than discussion of the boss' toupee. Or the freaking weather (which was slightly warmer than usual, but surprisingly, with some light snow).

Olivia's eyebrows furrowed for a split-second, almost imperceptibly. She held up a hand. "I solemnly promise to do my best to change the work culture for the better," she said as she looked everyone in the eye.

The group was surprised at the show of said solemnity. Lily went with it, and raised her glass, shouting, "To changing the culture!"

"To changing the culture," everyone clinked in return. Elizabeth, Jeremiah and Lily, enthusiastically; Mark and Shelia, reservedly.

"I'm relieved. For a second there, I thought you were going to go "Oh Captain My Captain" on us," Mark said.

Olivia grinned wickedly, with a gleam in her eye. "Well, I always loved Dead Poet's Society," she said as she climbed on the counter.

God, what is she doing? When the others registered this latest action of Olivia's, Lily cheered and Jeremiah made low sounds of approval. Shelia was slightly embarrassed, and hoped Olivia wouldn't make a fool of herself, and make a fool out of Shelia by association. Olivia wasn't even drunk!

"Hey everyone!" she shouted. The denizens of bar quieted their hum, curious at what announcement this imposing, but pretty, woman had to make. "I'm going to change some things at my workplace." she started. "I'm going to create a motherfucking POSITIVE culture, no matter what!" she yelled.

While confused about the context of this speech, the denizens of the bar nonetheless clapped good-naturedly at Olivia's enthusiastic announcement.

"C'mon, let's dance," Olivia proposed, on her return to the floor.

"I'm in," Lily said, following Olivia. Jeremiah shrugged and joined the two.

Shelia, Elizabeth, and Mark watched them go.

Elizabeth was shaking her head and smiling. "Wow, Olivia's an amazing character, isn't she? I wish I could be that brave." *Ugh, not her, too.* "Yeah, haha…" Shelia said absently. She took two more shots.

"Whoa there, easy girl," Mark said. Shelia rolled her eyes at him, and took another shot.

"It's Friday, and I'm going to relax and have fun," she said, defensively.

Mark held up his hands, signalling that he was backing off. After a pause, he switched gears by replying to Elizabeth's prior statement. "Olivia is certainly a character," he remarked. "But there's a fine line between courage and carelessness," he said definitively, taking a long drink. Elizabeth politely acknowledged the statement, but didn't say anything.

Jeremiah swung by, shouting, "You guys are missing all the fun! Come join us."

"I'm good for now," Shelia said.

"Bah, you're always "good for now!" Mark? Elizabeth?"

"I don't dance," Mark said, straight-faced.

"Of course you don't," Jeremiah sighed, with a smile. He raised an eyebrow up at Elizabeth.

"Oh, I'm not really that good at dancing," Elizabeth said abashedly.

"Neither am I. Except it's somehow worse because I'm black," he said sarcastically. "C'mon, it's fun making fools of ourselves," he said while holding out his hand.

"I never realized that being white gave me the advantage of having no expectations to dance well," she laughed. She took his hand, "Alright, count me in."

Shelia was intrigued by this turn of events. She watched them go to the dance floor. It turns out, they weren't kidding about being bad dancers. But she couldn't help but be heartened by how much fun all her coworkers seemed to be having. "I wonder if there's a romance brewing," she said, giggling maniacally, to her surprise.

Mark looked at Shelia, amused. "Well, what about your love life?" Mark asked.

Shelia took a swig of her drink. "What about it?"

Mark sighed. "You're not getting any younger, Shelia. I think you should put yourself out there."

Ouch. The last sign of anything remotely romantic happening in Shelia's life was half a year ago. This was a sore spot for her. But somehow less sore with the power of ethanol coursing through her veins. "You know what, Mark? I'm perfectly fine. You should mind your own business!" she said confidently. "Besides, it's harder because I have to sift through all these guys with Asian fetishes."

"Alright, alright. I was just grilling you because it's nice to have that special someone in your life, ya know?"

"Ha, it seems like that long-term relationship of yours has sheltered you from how treacherous the world of dating is." Mark sipped his drink. For a while the two just stood there, watching the others dancing. "I guess it true how they say Asians' faces go red when they're wasted."

"Fuck you," she said with a smirk.

Mark pretended to be offended. Another silence.

"Those guys are a sight, dancing next to all those teeny-boppers," he said.

Shelia considered his statement, surveying her coworkers on the dance floor. *Wow... That was an ambitiously bad dance move,* she thought, watching her coworkers in amazement. *But at least they're having fun.* "Yes, but it's kinda… nice. I think I'll join them. You might as well, too."

"I think not. But you do that," he said.

And do that, she did. Olivia and Lily welcomed her into their dancing circle enthusiastically, and Shelia boogied the night away. (She didn't throw up once.) She felt free.

She woke up with a great hangover. *Oh my god, why did I do that?* she groaned internally. She stayed in bed for a while. Hangover aside, she had to admit, she had a nice night. She felt like she broke new ground with her coworkers, for once, not feeling like she was merely putting on a Pleasant Participation mask with them.

But she still felt weird about life, in general. She was irked that she couldn't pinpoint why. *It can't just be that I'm hungover, right?* she thought hazily, falling asleep. When she got up, she moseyed on over to her bathroom. She looked at herself in the mirror. Out of habit she pinched a bit of muffin top and schemed about how to diet it off. She turned to her face: strong jawline, defined cheekbones, straight nose. *Thank God I don't have some obvious, ugly flaw. Then I really wouldn't know what to do with myself.* She pulled her eyelids down, then stretched out her cheeks while pursing her lips, willing her weirdness-about-life feeling to go away. *Isn't making faces supposed make me feel better or something?* She sighed, her face returning to its neutral glory.

She plopped down on her couch, resigning herself to zone out to some sitcom. As she reached for the remote, she noticed 'A Practical Guide to Life' right next to it. There was a slight layer of dust on it: it'd been a few weeks since she'd bought it. The book sat there, almost confrontational, accusing her of avoiding it (she hadn't been, she'd just forgotten about it. *Alright?*)

She grabbed it. She was surprised to see something sticking out within the pages, some blue paper that she hadn't noticed when she bought the book. She pulled it out.

From:
Candace Bell
6 Ogilvie Street
Surrey, British Columbia V5L 7H4
Canada

To:

Miss Moon
Rivercrest Retirement Facility
Ottawa, Ontario K1R 9V2
Canada

It was a torn open envelope; there was a letter inside.

Dear Mother,

I hope you're well. I wanted to update you on how our family is doing. Evan just turned 13. He's been doing really well at his Tae Kwon Do: he's two belts away from a black belt. And school, as always, is going excellently. Straight-A's again this year. Katie has shown a great interest in science, already. She loves to watch experiment videos on Youtube, and she cries hysterically when we have to pull her away from them! (Youtube is kind of like television, except on the internet.)

Things are still financially a bit difficult ever since George got laid off, but we're managing. As long as you keep in sight the important things in life, you can always be happy.

Love,
Candace

The letter was dated from two years ago. *Rivercrest facility, huh? I know where that is.* Shelia was curious for a moment by this development, but she was bored by the contents of the letter. She tossed it aside, and began reading the book.

WAKE THE FUCK UP

'You wake up. You're 40, 50, 60, whatever. Whatever age is it is that you realize that you spent your whole life going through the motions, putting the urgent over the important, never doing any of shit you actually fucking wanted to do, never stopping to smell the goddamn roses along the way. And you have 50% or less of your life left.'

Wow. Is this shit trying to prove something with all of its fancy swearing? Shelia thought, turning the page.

'Guess what, you miserable punk? It's not over for you yet. You're not fucking dead. And, you have some semblance of self-awareness, because you're reading this shit right now. Now, I'm not saying that reading my material = self-awareness, but the point is, by going out and buying a book like this, you took a small step in reversing years of force-fed stupidity in regards to your happiness. By wanting to change, a chunk of your work is already done. However. This is still a just a small step. Any idiot can read some shit, absorb maybe 1% of it or just forget the whole fucking thing, and go back to living their shitty lives. Knowledge without action is SHIT. So, I'll outline some fucking meaningful actions for you to take. I recommend that you do them. Otherwise you face a high risk of reading this crap, feeling inspired for a moment, and then forgetting about it and going back to your fucking automaton existence.'

Frankly, Shelia was offended. What did this—she flipped to the front cover...*Maria Walker* know of her life, her circumstances? There was a certain reality of needing money, needing to put food on the table. There was a certain reality of not being a failure. You couldn't just do whatever you wanted.

Fuck you, Maria Walker. She shoved the book aside.

Shelia had thought that night at the bar would have, like, magically made them all best friends or something. They would suddenly have deep, meaningful conversations. And live happily freaking after. *Why did I think that?* Everything was the same as before.

Well—some things were different. For example, Jeremiah and Elizabeth were a thing.

When she wasn't drunk, Shelia was not happy about being subjected to their love. At least, when she herself was not currently in a relationship. *I mean, are they trying to rub it in my face?*

And, of course, Olivia was no longer her "cubbie buddy". Shelia had gotten used to her relative absence after a couple of weeks. But obviously, Olivia was still around, trying to create a motherfucking positive culture.

And there were plants.

"Oh my god, Olivia," Lily exclaimed. "I love how you introduced all of these plants into the office. It makes this place seem so much more homey."

"Thanks Lily," Olivia said. "I agree. There's been studies that show that plants can boost worker's productivity and happiness."

"Oh, woow," Lily ahhed. Shelia could almost forgive Lily's fangirling as youthful enthusiasm, as she was five years' Shelia's junior. But then she resented the fact that someone so young had the same freaking pay grade as her.

"Well, what do you think of the new flora, Shelia?" Lily asked cheerfully.

"Well, um," Shelia considered what remark would earn her the most social capital. *They're marvellous! Bodacious! Cool!* "I didn't really notice the change I guess?" she mumbled. Today, she didn't have that much capacity for pretense. Lily and Olivia gave each other a knowing look.

"Oh my god, Shelia. You have to pay more attention to your surroundings, you know?" Lily said sincerely. Shelia looked between the two of them. *Oh. my. god. Indeed.* Shelia couldn't help herself—she snorted. Lily and Olivia didn't know what to make of this.

"Gosh, Lily, you're like an Olivia 2.0. Lucky us!" she said sarcastically. It felt good to let the lid off all that pent-up snark.

Olivia and Lily were shocked. "What's your problem?" Lily snapped.

Shelia continued on, drunk with destructiveness. "I'm just saying what we're all thinking," she said lightly. Lily was about to retort, but Olivia gently placed her hand on Lily, signalling a ceasefire. Lily nodded and went back to her cubicle.

"I think there's been a misunderstanding here. Shelia, will you come with me?" Olivia asked softly.

"Um, sure," she said. She got up and followed Olivia. Before, she would have been confused why Olivia wasn't pissed at her. Even slightly. But Shelia had gotten used to Olivia's ways.

Olivia led her to an area with windows, in front of a plant sitting on a ledge. The plant had recently been watered. "It's so pretty how the sunlight reflects the droplets," Olivia said.

"Mhm," Shelia said. Sheila didn't know what she was doing here. She shuffled uncomfortably as she waited for Olivia to say something, who was busy gazing out the window.

"Shelia, have you heard of the term mindfulness?" she finally said.

"Vaguely, here and there," she sighed, resigning herself to an Olivia Zen Talk. Normally she would have zoned out as soon as she recognized a zen talk coming, but today she gave in.

"Well, it's basically… paying attention to what's going on around you. Not thinking about what you had for breakfast, or…" Olivia racked her brains. "Or an upcoming dental appointment, or that thing you said wrong, or whatever! It's focusing on what's happening right now. The pressure of your heartbeat, the waning of a shadow, the stranger with the sad eyes you pass by every morning." Olivia paused. "I think that's what Lily was trying to get at."

Shelia looked at Olivia. She darted her eyes away when Olivia looked back. Staring at the ground, she grudgingly said, "I didn't know you were a poet."

"You think you would have known someone has poetic tendencies after you work with them for two years," Olivia said, smiling. "You know, they talk about mindfulness in 'A Practical Guide to Life'. They have some exercises for it too. Like, staring at something for a period of time." A lightbulb visibly flashed across her face when she said, "I know! Why don't you look at this plant for a whole minute, without thinking about anything but what is being presented to you?"

Shelia regarded the plant. "I think I'll pass."

"Is getting away from your thoughts really such a radical thing?" she said. "What's the harm in trying?"

Shelia crossed her arms. She could physically feel an unpleasantness coursing through her that would inevitably latch onto others unless she put a lid on it.

She endeavoured to get away from Olivia. "Uh, well, I could be working. So I'll just go back to that now," she said, as she turned away.

"Right, you mean playing Monkey Quest?" Olivia rolled her eyes. "You know, you always shut things down before you give them a chance," Olivia said behind her.

I guess she found out how much time I waste on asinine Facebook games. Olivia's bait was too tempting a target for Shelia's spite. She stopped walking and turned to face Olivia.

"That's not true. I read that book you recommended, and by the way, *it's terrible.*"

"Right. You probably read the first page and gave up because it offended your sensibilities," Olivia said coolly. Shelia could not admit Olivia's accuracy, even to herself. She kept her expression neutral. She said, "I'm not going to waste my time reading something that is completely unrealistic. I read it, and it sucked. You can't say I didn't give it a chance." Olivia scrutinized Shelia's face, as if looking for something. "Actually, I can," she said sadly. Finding nothing, she walked away.

Damnit, she got the last word. Shelia was left with the bitter aftertaste of conflict.

Shelia's heated exchanges left her feeling unsettled. She had felt powerful, finally expressing her thoughts: but why were her thoughts so bitchy? The drunken destructiveness that had fuelled her behaviour vanished, leaving only the weight of her transgressions. (What could be considered a transgression in the buttoned-up small-talk office world, anyway.)

Shelia took care to avoid Olivia and Lily. This was difficult as there was only one main route in and out of the building, so at closing time Shelia had to hang around until they left. She hovered by the water station: an alibi should anyone question what she was doing. She saw Olivia, Lily, and Mark talking and laughing, lingering by the doors. *C'mon, hurry up and leave*, she thought, tapping her foot. She was so, so, grateful that it was the long weekend. Maybe the unpleasantness would blow over the next time she saw them.

In the distance, Shelia watched Jeremiah pick up a fallen flower from one of the potted plants, and give it to Elizabeth. Elizabeth smiled and put it in her hair.
Jesus, I'm surrounded by hippies.
Shelia was alarmed to see Jeremiah had spotted her and was making his way over. She hastily got a drink of water.

"Hey Shelia. Whatcha hanging around here for? It's the long weekend!"

"Oh, you know, just staying hydrated…" she said sing-songily. "What about you?"

"Me and Elizabeth, we tinkered with some of the models and created a new program," Jeremiah said, gesturing to Elizabeth, working away at her computer. "We think it'll really revolutionize things. I can't wait to show it at the next meeting," Jeremiah said.

"Wow. Dedication."

"What are your plans for this weekend?" he asked good-
naturedly.

"I'm heading to Waterloo to visit my parents," Shelia said.

"Sounds like fun."

2

It was a welcome, five hour drive from Ottawa to Waterloo;
full of speeding for thrill, zoning out to her finely curated
playlist, and stopping for snackage at convenience stores.

She pulled into her parents' driveway around noon. Every
time she visited, the taupe colour of the house reminded her
of their poor design sense. *Why didn't they go with a nice
maroon, or stucco?* she lamented. She noticed that her sister's
beaten up '06 Chevrolet had already gotten there.

"Hello Shi-lei," her mother said as she hugged her and
planted a kiss on her cheek. Her mother looked as she usually
did, soft face with faint lines. Shelia hugged her back.

"Where's Dad? And is Mei here?" she asked.

The said Mei popped up beside her mother. "Yo," said Mei,
coming in for a hug. Her younger sibling had her usual look:
outfitted trendily with a hint of bohemian elements, hair past
the shoulders, winged eyeliner that added some sharpness to
her round visage. Shelia noticed that her sister's fiancé, John,
was also there.

"Hey Shelia," John greeted, when Shelia and Mei pulled
back.

"Hey John. I didn't know you were coming. It's nice to see you," Shelia said.

"You too."

Mei had had several boyfriends before John. They were usually white, like John, and Shelia had been wary of all of them (white and non-white alike.) They were either potheads, or chewed with their mouths open, or listened to country music or dubstep, or did some other, unforgivable thing. But John was normal and agreeable. Shelia was relieved that Mei had finally found a suitable mate, but her younger sister getting married before her was a hard pill to swallow.

I'm genuinely happy for Mei, Shelia silently repeated.

"Your father is out getting groceries. You've come from a long drive, go and wash your face and eat!" her mother prodded.

"Alright, alright." She plopped down her bag and went upstairs.

"Shelia, we're just watching Dreary McGee. Come join us when you're done," Mei said.

Dreary McGee was one of those sitcoms that Shelia hated for its fluffiness but would still watch if it was on. She inexplicably found herself laughing along with John and Mei. The credits rolled by, and Mei shut off the television.

"Do you want to go for a walk by the river with us Sheel?" Mei asked.

"Nah," Shelia said. *I'd rather be a lazy fuck for a bit.*

"Alright. See you in a bit Shelia," John said, and off they went. In their absence, Shelia sat slumped on her couch, wondering what to do with herself. Her default activity when she didn't know what to do would be to a) Do some work she inevitably had to do b) Check Emails or c) Watch TV. But with this break from her usual environment, her default was reset. She blanked and wondered: why was she was at her parents' house, anyway?

To spend some quality time with them before they inevitably die at some point. Her usual barrage of thoughts slowed down and made way for this particular thought, which settled uncomfortably into her consciousness.

"Why the hell do I depress myself so much?" she muttered aloud.

Shelia made her way to the kitchen. Her mom was cooking dumplings.

"Dumplings huh? Must be a special occasion," Shelia joked.

"Yes, dinners with our future son-in-law are very special occasions," her mom replied.
Shelia feigned incredulousness. "But, what about the special occasion of your only daughters visiting?"

"Yes, yes, that too," she said dismissively. Shelia rolled her eyes and sneaked a dumpling into her mouth.

"Those are for dinner, Shi-lei."

Shelia watched her mother do her thing for a bit. "Can I help?" she asked. Her mom gave her the go-ahead, and Shelia picked up some dough and started folding. Shelia found herself lost in repetitive motion: rolls and folds and filling, rolls and folds and filling...

It was nice.

"Try folding it like this," her mother demonstrated. "It'll make it easier."

Shelia copied her technique. "Ohhhhhhh," she said, smiling. She was officially converted to her mother's Way of Folding the Dumplings.

Shelia, however, did eventually revert to TV and checking emails. She asked her mother for the Wi-Fi password. She didn't know it. Her father came back, arms a-full with groceries. Shelia filled him on on the usual: Ottawa's was weather was bad, her job was going fine. He supplied her with the password, which was something convoluted like bGh653rew1.

A couple of hours later, John and Mei came back.

"Long walk," Shelia commented.

"Yeah, John and I went to the museum and then to a café afterwards," Mei explained.

Her parents were in the midst of setting the table. "You are all just in time for dinner," her mom said, as she placed chopsticks for every plate except one. (The lonely cutlery were presumably for John.)

"Ms. Yang, I don't need those anymore," John said triumphantly. "I've got the chopstick technique down. See?" he said, while demonstrating his new skills.

Her father beamed and patted him on the back. "Well done," he said. Her mother gave him the thumbs-up. Mei grinned, amused. Shelia resisted the urge to roll her eyes. *Sure, get an in with your fiancée's Asian parents by mastering chopstick use.*

The dinner itself was heaven. Shelia lost track of the outside world and could only be found in the stir fry, braised pork, wontons, and of course, dumplings. Signs of the outer world would sometimes surface, like murmurings of "This dish is fantastic," or, "The economy these days…"

Soon, her mind registered that persons were trying to contact her.

"So, Shelia?" Mei asked impatiently.

Shelia blinked. "Uh… what?"

"We were wondering if you meet any nice man in Ottawa yet," her mom said.

Goddamnit. I was in a nice mood. She cleared her throat and said lightly, "No, not yet."

Her parents' faces crinkled with concern. "Shelia, you're getting older. You must settle down soon," her father remarked.

Shelia wished this conversation was happening in Chinese, not English, so that at least John wouldn't get a chance to comment on her spinsterhood. "I get it. But don't worry about me. There's plenty of guys out there," Shelia said, as pleasantly as she could. She felt like running out of there.

Mei and John shot each other a look.

"You know, Shelia, I know a guy in Ottawa. His name is Dipon, and I think you two would get along," John said as he wrote this stranger's number on a napkin. Shelia considered whether she should scathingly reply that she didn't need anybody's pity help.

"Shi-lei, I think you should contact this man," her mom said eagerly.

Shelia suppressed the snark—and a sigh. "Thank you, John. I'll consider calling him."

Shelia wished she were back in her food reverie. Now she felt irritated. And hyper-aware of the ensuing silence, which was marked by the usual dinner noises.

Her mother took a shot at breaking it up. "John, what is your opinion on retirement homes?"

"Retirement homes? What about them?"

She took a minute to gather her words. Finally, she said, "You see, in North America there is a different attitude towards the elderly. In China, when the mom and dad grow old, they live with the children. But here, they get stuck in retirement home. Children do not visit much. It strikes me as very sad."

John considered her thoughts. "Hmm. I think it's because the West values independence very much. The children's independence, and I imagine, the parents' as well. Although, I do think that children should visit more often," he said diplomatically.

Mei chewed her food thoughtfully. Shelia wondered if Mei saw that their mother was testing John for down-the-road matters. *Well played, Ma.*

Shelia settled into her room. She picked it strategically: as far as possible from Mei and John's rooms so that she could avoid overhearing, ahem, nightly activity. She was glad that her parents had moved out of her childhood home, because if she was in her old bedroom it would probably conjure up old memories, and she wasn't in the mood for nostalgia.

Unfortunately, thinking that she didn't want to think about the past automatically made her brain think about the past. Specifically: when exactly did she fuck up her life?

Growing up, she had worked hard throughout her school career, to match the incredible work ethic her parents had to have in order to come here. Her mother worked as a treasurer at an engineering company and her father as an engineer. Shelia planned to become an engineer, too, from an early age. In secondary school she befriended like-minded go-getters and was well on her way. However, Shelia never thought about whether she actually liked engineering. She suffered through her degree only to find out engineering didn't suddenly become more enjoyable once you started working.

She decided not to dwell on this too much and to accept that this was her reality. After all, working hard at something she wasn't passionate about had been her modus operandi for all her life. Most people didn't love their jobs, and this was just how society was. They made ends meet, tried to make the non-working hours count, and lived their lives.

She and her boyfriend, a guy she bonded with over the stress of the engineering, had moved in together shortly after graduation. Parker, the boyfriend in question, seemed unperturbed by the working world. Shelia tried to be as OK-with-everything as Parker, but the increasing feeling of listlessness as a few years rolled by won over. She had, finally, after working towards it for the majority of her life, officially "arrived" at her "real life", and all she could think was, *Was this it?*

~

"Of course it's not it, dummy. Parker's your first boyfriend. You guys will outgrow each other and move on," Mei rolled her eyes. She was still doing her Bachelor of Arts in Toronto at the time, and she was visiting for the spring break.

Shelia felt that this was needlessly harsh. All that agonizing to admit her life was not together, only to be met with mockery by her little sister. "Parker is not the problem. We've been together for six years. Our relationship is perfectly fine."

"Just fine?" Mei asked, emphasizing 'fine'.

"Mei, things are not like how they are in the movies, okay? They set up unrealistic expectations which cause people to be blind to the perfectly fine things they have already," Shelia said, exasperated.

Mei snorted. "This, coming from Miss Experienced With Relationships."

"At least I've had a relationship last longer than a week," Shelia retorted.

"I've had relationships last longer than a week," Mei muttered. "Alright. So if Parker isn't the problem, then what is?"

Could the problem really just be that she didn't like her job? It seemed much bigger than that. Impossible to pin down. Shelia shrugged and stared at the floor.

Shelia and Parker suddenly had way more money than they knew what to with. So, naturally, they'd bought a house and a fancier car. Shelia felt like she was playing a twisted version of 'Grown Up', and all that was missing was the 2.0 kids.

Shelia hugged her pillow. She stared at Parker's exposed back, gently moving up and down with each inhale and exhale. It was another one of those times when she'd said, "Not tonight." She had kissed his cheek to lessen the sting of rejection. Lately, she was never in the mood. Quarter-life crises, it turns out, mess up your sex life.

She woke up with Parker facing her. He was absent-mindedly playing with her hair.

"Morning," he smiled.

She made a murmuring sound in response.

"I was thinking," he said, as he put on his work shirt, "Do you want to go for dinner later?"

"Um," She registered Parker's question. It took longer than normal because Shelia wasn't expecting it. Usually, they had their own little morning routines, during which they spoke to each other only if strictly necessary, like to ask if one knew where the other's razor was.

"Yeah, sure," she mumbled.

"Great," he said. He pecked her cheek and left. *How the hell is he so chipper at 6 in the morning,* she thought foggily. She was glad her work started slightly later.

In between consulting the company's client, AMC Construction, Shelia texted Parker.

   : So, where are we going?
Parker: Pierro Blanco Chateau.
     : Wow. Fancy.
Parker: yup! :)
     : Alright, see you later.

Shelia felt wary. Why was he taking her out to fancy dinners all of a sudden? *It wouldn't be to... propose, would it?* They'd already had that conversation. After Shelia and Parker had been together for four years, when they were twenty-three, Parker had asked Shelia what she thought of the whole marriage and kids deal.

Specifically, he'd asked, "What do you think of going from Ms. Yang to Mrs. Choi? And like, you know, little versions of us running around, one day?"

Shelia had blanked at the question. *Marriage? Kids? Changing my name?!* She hadn't considered if she wanted those things, wanted those things with Parker. So she had provided a default response. "I think it would be the logical next step, way down the road," she said cautiously.

"It's interesting how you describe matters of the heart as 'logical next steps'," Parker noted, but he didn't press the issue then.

Shelia thought she should have been honest then and said she didn't know. *Then I might not be in this mess.* She printed up some blueprints, and returned to the client.

Later, the two were back from work and were getting ready to go to Pierro Blanco Chateau. She hated having to think about her outfit. She wished formal dressing up was as simple as choosing her work outfit: Button-up, slacks, done.

She decided on a stupid black dress, and squeezed some earrings in her ears. (If she wore them for more than a few hours, she was going to get a crazy allergic reaction, and it would not be pretty.)

"Wow, you look great."

"You too," she said.

Parker was about to head out, but Shelia lingered, hesitatingly.

"Sheel? You ready?" he asked. Shelia paused. *I should just confront him about it before he asks… Or will that make things awkward?*

"Yeah. Coming," she said. Her unvoiced concerns sat in her, heavy.

She stayed pensive throughout the drive to the restaurant. They pulled into the parking lot, went in, and were seated. Shelia noted big-ass chandeliers dotting the ceiling. *This place is trying so hard to be fancy.*

"Halibut, please," Parker said.

"Burger for me," Shelia said flatly. And then they waited. Shelia started tapping her fingers. *Why are formal dinners a thing? It seems so contrived. Coffee is better,* she thought.

"So, how was work today?" Parker asked.

Nooooo, why would he ask that? Shelia groaned before he even finished the question.

"What?" Parker asked, alarmed.

"I absolutely cannot do small talk right now," she said, fed up.

Parker seemed hurt. "It's a fairly standard question. I can tell you about how my day went, if you'd prefer that…"

"No. I don't care."

Now Parker seemed fed up. "Wow. That's so considerate of you, honey," he said sarcastically.

"Look. We just got back from working all day. Why should we talk about it in our downtime?"

"Because it's interesting work," he said.

"No, it's not," she said boorishly.

Parker crossed his arms. "Alright, why don't you suggest a topic, if talking about your job distresses you so much?"

Shelia sighed. She may have inadvertently found a solution to her problem—be so much of an annoying bitch that your boyfriend won't propose to you even if he was planning on it.

"Okay, um." She looked up at the ceiling, as if to pray to the fancy chandelier gods. "Why are we doing this? It seems so out of the blue. You're not going to, you know…" she couldn't say it.

"What?" Parker pressed.

"…Propose?" Shelia managed.

Parker raised his eyebrows. He was flabbergasted. "No, I wasn't going to…What gave you that idea? Uh, I mean, do you want…me to?"

"No!" Shelia practically screamed.

Parker was quiet for a moment. Slowly, he said, "Well… why not?"

Shelia took a breath, willing herself to get through this conversation. "Because, I'm not sure if I want what it entails. Kids, and settling down… I'm not sure if I'm ready for it."

"That's what you said when I asked you ages ago. Are you really not sure you want those things, or are you not sure you want those things with me?" he asked quietly.

Shelia shut her eyes. Now she realized why she was so nervous about this dinner—because of *this*. "Parker, don't be like that! That's not what I meant," she pleaded.

Parker furrowed his eyebrows. His expression was taut. Just then, their dinner arrived. The steam rose off the plates, creating a buffer around the troubled lovers.

The waiter didn't pick up on the tense atmosphere between Shelia and Parker, so he engaged them in light conversation. As Parker had become too moody for manners, Shelia humoured the waiter, painfully, trying to keep herself sociable. As soon as he left, her affable smile vanished.

"Parker… I don't understand why you're so upset. You weren't even going to propose," she pointed out.

"Yeah, but, it's going to come up sooner or later! Shelia, we're twenty-five," he said, exasperated. "It's not exactly like we're spring chickens."

"Twenty-five seems pretty young to me," she said off-handedly. "Okay… if you weren't going to propose, then why did you do this dinner? We don't normally do this."

Parker sighed. "I don't know, I wanted to, rekindle the romance I guess. I noticed you never want to, you know…"

"Have sex. Right," she said, embarrassed. "It's not you," she insisted. "It's me. I'm weird right now."

Parker searched her face, as if looking for some hidden meaning. He stared at his plate, frowning.

Shelia picked off her bun and poured some extra sauce on the burger before neatly placing the bun back. "Um, you know, I appreciate you doing all of this, but formal dinners aren't really my thing," she said.

"Noted."

They awkwardly chewed their food. "This food is pretty good, though," Shelia offered. Parker nodded.

They ate the rest of their meal in silence.

After that, Shelia and Parker relationshipped as normal, but there was a sense that something was off.

Shelia plopped a sugar cube into her tea, during their weekend morning tea routine. Parker stirred his cup slowly, in deep thought. He cleared his throat.

"I don't think…this is working," he said quietly, staring at his tea.

Shelia shut her eyes. She could will herself to believe what was happening wasn't happening; she could prolong the inevitable by saying, *What do you mean?* A tear made a small splash into her teacup. She opened her eyes, and nodded. She saw that Parker's eyes were wet too.

Breaking up, predictably, hurt like a bitch. Shelia felt that the worst thing was the feeling of being unanchored, set so loose upon the world that she might float away from it. She'd spent her formative early twenties with this guy. Without the relationship, she was strange to herself.

She was grateful for the job that she didn't like because it kept her busy, her mind busy. She also was lucky that it was fall, AKA new episode season, so she could further distract herself.

One day, after two months of wallowing, Mei called, bearing an opportunity. "Sheel. You've broken up with your boyfriend of millennia, which means you need a major change, and you hate your job."

Shelia sighed. "Okay..."

"And you're a decent programmer... and you actually like programming... So, why don't you come work for Keegan's brother's company? It's in Ottawa, and they desperately need coders."

With Mei's offer, gears started turning in Shelia's head. She hadn't considered that she could actually do something about her drudgery. For some reason, she couldn't immediately show that her interest was piqued, so she said, dryly, "Your boyfriend's brother? Won't it be awkward for me when you guys break up?"

"Shelia! Don't be such a bitch. I'm trying to help you," Mei said, annoyed.

~

Shelia smirked, momentarily distracted from her rumination of the past—she'd forgotten about Roy, Keegan's brother. Mei and Keegan had eventually broken up, and it had been indeed awkward whenever she passed by Roy in the hallways. He quit a few months after their break-up, and Shelia had no idea what he was doing now.

~

"Alright, alright, sorry. Um..." Shelia hesitated. "That actually sounds good? What should I do?"
Mei relayed to her the details. The company (aka Cogville) was impressed with a program she'd coded for her engineering job, and hired her on the spot.

~

Shelia'd forgotten that she'd once hated a job more than the one she currently had. *Actually... I did use to like this Cogville job. But then I guess things got really routine after a while.*
With all that reminiscing, did she figure out where she went wrong in life? She thought about it.
Nope. Her mind recalled the dinner conversation, and everyone's stupid, disappointed, judgemental faces at the face of her singledom. Since her break-up with Parker, she'd been on a few dates via online dating sites. After a plethora of dud dates and meaningless sex, Shelia'd given up on online

dating, and it seems, dating in general, since she hadn't been on anymore since she quit half a year ago. *I'm not even sure what's worse, bad sex, or no sex.* She couldn't shake the feeling that she was a complete and utter loser.

A tear from each eye made their way onto her cheeks. She went to sleep.

Before Shelia, Mei, and John left Waterloo, they all went for a walk by the river.

"Nothing can beat the Rideau canal, though," as she said it, Shelia realized she hadn't actually gone to the canal that much in the two years she lived in Ottawa.

She slowed her pace to match her parents'. Mei and John were walking slightly ahead, hand-in-hand. Mei turned her head and said, "Wow, already speaking like an Ottawa native, as if you didn't grow up here! Traitor!" she laughed.

"Ha."

"Shelia, one day we will visit, and you can show your mother and I around Ottawa."

"Sure. Sounds great," Shelia said. *As long as you don't pester me about my lame love life.*

They walked in silence. Shelia watched the river. *Wow. Sunset over the water.* For a while, the only things she thought about were the novel colours of the sky. They seemed to wash over her and cleanse her of her burdens.

Later, back at the house, she hugged everyone goodbye, and drove back with a lighter heart.

Her heart returned to its usual weight Monday morning. Shelia was slightly afraid to face Olivia and Lily. She stopped just before the metal entrance doors, debating internally what her course of action should be. *Hmm. Maybe if I apologized it would smooth over the awkwardness.*

Why should I apologize? It's not like I said or did anything that was that bad.

Who cares? It's just to ease office relations.

Well, maybe it will blow over. For today I should just do my best to avoid them. That way I don't have to apologize over dumb shit. It was decided, then: her course of action would be to avoid the hell out of Olivia and Lily. Once she got to work, it was easy enough to do. It's not like the two went out of their way to interact with Shelia.

"Where you heading off to, Shelia? Lunchroom's that way," Mark commented during break, noticing Shelia was walking in a different direction.

Shelia decided to be proactive about her avoidance and stay clear of the building during lunchtime. "Just going for a walk. Fresh air, you know?"

"Alright. See you."

Once she opened the door, a gentle breeze greeted her. She actually hadn't gone for a walk around her work in such a long time. *I should visit the Rideau Canal sometime, too,* she vowed. She put her hands in her pockets and strolled at a leisurely pace, surveying the concrete jungle around her. The people she passed by were different from the five o'clock crowd of employees she was used to. There were more elderly, children, and a few teenagers skipping school.

She made her way to the surprisingly cheap phở place she visited millennia ago, musing at its almost art-like rundownness. Through the window, she watched people go while she sipped her noodles, wondering about their lives. She noted a couple who looked like an older version of her parents.

Glancing at her phone, she saw the time was 12:37. She had to be back at 12:40. "Shit," she said out loud, mouth full of noodles. The waitress looked at her questioningly.

"Oh, uh, don't worry about it," Shelia smiled hastily. She gobbled up the last of her phở, slammed some cash on the counter (tip: 20 percent), and ran out the door.

She slid into her seat huffing, and carried out her programming duties for the rest of the day with ease.

The next day, there was a meeting. Shelia, personally, didn't know why meetings were a thing because everyone seemed to dislike them.

The boss, Steve, stood at the head of the table with a severe look on his face. Shelia was the only one who seemed to notice, as everyone else was busy chatting.

Steve cleared his throat. "I'm afraid I have some bad news, everyone." If Steve had happened to be wearing a hat, he would have taken it off gravely at this point. "This isn't a decision I've taken lightly, but in order to keep the company afloat and keep most of the jobs in the long-run, this is, I'm afraid, necessary…" The coworkers exchanged worried glances with each other. Shelia just waited for the ball to drop. Steve sighed. "Within the next month, we're going have to reduce the workforce by 30 percent."

There was stunned silence in which people slowly registered what was happening, and then, an outburst of disappointment.

"Oh my god," Elizabeth said sadly, who was sitting next to Shelia. Her hands were clasped around her mouth, and the front of her eyebrows were arched upwards. There were similar expressions on everyone else.

Shelia was dumbfounded. She always thought she would leave the company eventually, but now that the company could be doing that work for her, she didn't know what to feel. But what she did feel was massively unprepared. Sure, she'd known the economy was technically in the pits, but it hadn't seemed to affect things at Cogville. *I mean, Olivia even got promoted.*

"Now, anyone who is laid off will get a severance package, and we will do our best to help you find other jobs…"

Nobody seemed to be listening at this point; they were all reeling in their minds.

There was a sense of dejection as everyone walked out of the meeting. Olivia turned to face them.

"Guys. I know this is a lot to take in, but I wanted to let you know that no matter what happens, we'll get through this. If I myself am still around… I'll have regular meet ups where we can discuss the job market and available openings, for anyone who's—who's going to be directly affected." Olivia had the look of utmost sincerity. It was very comforting to people.

"Thanks, Olivia," Elizabeth said quietly.

"Yeah, I'm sure it would be much appreciated," Jeremiah said.

Shelia nodded, forgetting for a moment that Olivia and her were sort of on bad terms.

"I'm really worried," Lily said, quickly wiping her tears. Olivia gave her a hug, and Elizabeth put a reassuring arm on her shoulder.

Shelia didn't feel like discussing this latest happening with people, so she slipped away stealthily. Mark still noticed her, though.

"So. You OK?"

Shelia shrugged, morosely.

So…I guess this is probably karma, or whatever, Shelia thought as she walked out of the familiar metal doors, for possibly one of the last times. *With me always bitching about my job.* She didn't normally subscribe to higher powers such as karma, the universe, or god(s), but in desperate times, sometimes believing that inalienable forces were fucking up your life was better than believing that it was due to plain randomness. It massaged the fact that one was a meaningless speck in the cosmos, ever-hurtling towards death.

Shelia sighed. Now she was going to be a spinster and possibly unemployed. *Okay, time to get shitfaced.*

Shelia could worry about the stigma of drinking alone, but she brushed those concerns aside. She decided to go to a pub called Feehan's. On the way, she stopped, realizing she was in front of Olivia's mythical fish store, the water in the fish tanks reflecting back a warped version of her face. A long, silvery fish glided ethereally before her. She wiggled her finger at the glass. A skinny little thing came to see what was up, and then flitted away. "Bye, little guy," she said. *Olivia was right, all those years ago. This place is pretty relaxing.*

She arrived at Feehan's. The door was hidden around the corner, almost like an afterthought. She slipped in, the lighting about the same level as the post-sunset light outside. Rumblings of conversation filled the air. Feehan's was one of those pubs with an open window, so you could reach out and touch passersby if you felt inclined. Shelia ordered some food and a drink and settled onto the stool, surveying the street scene outside. She felt a little insecure. *Maybe I should have brought a notebook or laptop, pretend to work on something.* An old dude on the sidewalk whistled at her.

She flipped him off. After the distasteful feeling subsided, she swivelled her stool away from the street and leaned her elbow on the counter, looking at the inside. *Okay, act like you're not insecure, at least.*

Shelia eavesdropped on a conversation between two friends, a punk and a goth.

"I got an A in all of my classes, except for Geophysics, where I got a B," said the goth, a petite girl, disappointedly.

"Nice," said the punk, a skinny, pale dude. "I'm still waiting on my English 224 mark. I'm pretty nervous."
Shelia was intrigued by how boring their conversation was. *Don't stress so much about your grades, it matters less than you think,* she wanted to tell them. The waitress, a delicately pretty girl with an afro, brought over her order.

"Waiting for someone?" she asked amicably.

"No," Shelia forced a smile. "Thanks." She guzzled half her drink and seemed to inhale a chunk of her fries. She turned her attention to two people sitting at a table near Shelia.

"Oh yah, I'm pretty excited for James' party," the tan blonde woman said.

"Yeah? I hear his brother is coming back after being abroad for three years," said rugged outdoorsy white dude (i.e beard, flannel). Shelia wondered, *Friends? Lovers?*

"Wow. That's a long time," the woman commented. Beard dude nodded. They sipped their drink simultaneously.

"So, how's your brother doing?" he asked. *Dude definitely likes her, but the chick is ambivalent right now,* Shelia decided.

Blondie sighed. "Uh, better, I guess. To be honest, we don't really talk much. We… don't have a great relationship. Even before he got an addiction, we didn't," she said, pursing one side of her lips downward. The guy nodded sympathetically. In a sort of meta-musing, she thought what she would think of herself, sitting at a barstool all alone. Probably, *"Look at that sad, pathetic, loser."*

Or, maybe I'd be easier on myself. After all, I don't know why I'm sitting here. Maybe I'd imagine some tragic scenario, like a great lover dying. Or, like, my company announcing lay-offs.

I'm not technically laid off. Why am I acting like it, anyway? Maybe to take the shock off once it actually happens.

Shouldn't I be researching other jobs then?

Shelia nibbled at her fries. It occurred to her that she could be happy about this. *I do hate my job. This could be the push I needed.*

A slow trickle of people came in, steadily livening the atmosphere. *But I'm worried about staying afloat. It's gonna be hard to find another job in this economy. And, if I find one, what if I don't like it like all of my other jobs?* Shelia ate her food, slowly, but refilled her drink quite a few times. She lost track of the time, enthralled listening to people's sagas.

A giggling fit escaped from her, garnering some pointed looks from surrounding people, but she didn't care. *My face is probably red now.* This hypothesis was confirmed when she took a look at her reflection in her glass.

"Ha!" she said, pointing at it.

She finally finished her meal and wandered outside, the sky considerably darker than when she first came in. She took care to walk normally, but the stumbles occasionally emerged. She passed by partygoers dressed in sexy outfits, homeless folk, and one or two wandering, uncategorizable people. Like herself perhaps. The lights were predictably off in all the stores, except for faint glows from bars. One establishment stood out like a sore thumb, and that was Yoyo's Books. The lights were on, it was open, and it was almost 2 am. A bastion in the darkness. *I'm a human-moth drawn to the light,* she thought, heading towards Yoyo's.

The familiar bell tinkled behind her. "Hi Yoyo," Shelia said, waving maniacally.

Yoyo looked up from her book and raised her eyebrows.

"Do you remember me?" Shelia asked, slightly slurred.

"It's hard to forget a person who buys 'A Practical Guide to Life'," she said wryly. "Did you figure out your life yet?"

"I don't think so," Shelia said honestly. She poked the 'Death and Taxes' rubber chicken, and it emitted a drawn-out squeaky noise.

Yoyo exhaled. "Alright. Well, let's get you some tea." She hobbled out from behind the counter. This surprised Shelia, because Yoyo almost seemed too blunt to be old, and have old-people problems like trouble walking. She led Shelia towards the back and around the corner, revealing a hidden area of tables and bookshelves. There were rundown-looking men playing chess, reading, and of course, drinking tea. They took note of Shelia, as she was a bit of an oddity there, but then they went back to their business. Shelia took a seat while Yoyo went off to presumably make said tea.

She placed Shelia's cup on the table with a bit of force, like a gritty bartender slamming down a shot glass. Yoyo took her seat across from Shelia, sipping her tea.

"You know, if a Native man walks in drunk, the cops get called. Probably rough him up. A cute little Asian girl like yourself does it, and I'd bet my ass no one would give a shit," she mused.

"Hey. I'm not a cute little Asian girl, I'm a grown-ass woman," Shelia said. She snorted trying to restrain an errant fit of giggles, to no use. Yoyo looked amused.

"Why are you open at 2 AM, anyway? Wouldn't the only people who come in be, like, drunk?" Shelia asked, still kind of giggling.

"You'd be surprised how much business comes from drunk people at 2 AM," Yoyo smiled. "Which reminds me. You better buy something before leaving," Yoyo said mischievously.

"Fine. But don't sell me crap like 'A Practical Guide to Life'. It's terrible," Shelia said. She sniffed a single, long, sniff.

"Ap-parent-ly!" Yoyo drew out. "Because it seems like your life still isn't sorted out, is it?" Yoyo chuckled.

Yoyo reminded Shelia of her sister. Specifically, the criticizing-of-life-choices part. She had a vision of senior-citizen Mei, quietly forever-mocking Shelia until death was thrust upon one or the other sister.

"So, what's the problem, girly?" Yoyo asked kindly, perceiving Shelia's glum expression.

Shelia drank some tea. "Lemon ginger?" she asked. Yoyo nodded.

"Um. Okay," Shelia tried. "Well, I might lose my job. Also, I'll probably die alone."

Put into words, Shelia thought her problems may have seemed a little trite. Especially in front of Yoyo, and surrounded by people who were probably homeless. *I mean, Yoyo looks like she's seen some shit.* But expressing her demons took the power away from them, and Shelia felt relieved.

Yoyo nodded, seemingly not thinking Shelia's problems were trivial. "Okay. You fear your worst case scenario. Broke and alone. Makes sense to me," she grunted. "So, let's say the worst case comes true. What are you gonna do?"

Shelia shrugged cartoonishly. Yoyo put her hand to her face, and rubbed her forehead.

"Missy, you have to confront your issues. How are you going to get through them if you don't even think about them? Think about it now. You lose your job tomorrow. How long will your rainy-day fund last you?"

Even while inebriated, Shelia could do mental math like nobody's business. *Omg azns r so gud at m4th.* Shelia smiled, recalling an online chat conversation back in high school making fun of "positive racial stereotypes". She considered her finances.

"About four months," Shelia said.

Yoyo whistled. "That's a lot of time to figure out your shit, girly. You've got it good," she smiled.

Shelia burped. She covered her mouth, laughing. "The economy is so bad though," she giggled. "I don't think I can find another job."

Yoyo scoffed. "I've been around a long time, and let me tell you, the economy is always 'bad'. Yet people still manage. You'll be okay," Yoyo said. "If you really can't find a job, you might consider being your own boss. Though let me tell you, it ain't for the faint of heart. I've fallen on rough patches a coupl'a times. More than a coupl'a times, actually," Yoyo said as an afterthought, "All this online shoppin' ain't helping either. But can't say I blame people, seems pretty convenient," she shrugged. She continued, "You see, I've created a community here, and we help each other out."

Shelia nodded. She could see that.

"Okay, so, ummm. What about my failed love life?" Shelia asked.

Yoyo thought about it. "So. Say no one ever loves you, romantically at least, for the rest of your life. What are you going to do about it?"

"Be... miserable, I guess?"

"Well, that's that." Yoyo said definitively.

Shelia was surprised by the finality of the discussion. "That's that." Shelia echoed mournfully, drinking her tea.

Yoyo shook her head, laughing. "It's a valid option, but just so ya know, not being miserable is too. Why not have an awesome life, whether ya've got a plus one or not?"

"Because a good life isn't possible without one?"

"Says you," Yoyo said, raising her eyebrows.

"Says everyone," Shelia muttered.

"Screw them!" she cackled.

"But what if they're your friends and family?"

"All the more reason. Listen, hun, there's a skill you should learnt'a cultivate. It's called not giving a crap about what people think of ya," Yoyo stood up, and patted her on the back. "You should get some sleep. I assume you have work tomorrow?"

"Yeah…" she sighed, as she got up as well.

Yoyo stood with her hands on her hips, considering Shelia's face. "Seems like you don't even like your job that much. If I were you, with that much time to find an income, I'd just quit instead of waiting for the ball the drop."

"That's impractical," Shelia whispered, yawning. "Where are these guys going to go when you close?" Shelia asked as she turned the hidden corner, headed for the door. Some of the said guys noticed Shelia was leaving and waved goodbye. "Bye, young lady!" one of the chess players said. She waved back.

"Most of 'em stay. I give them sleeping bags."

Shelia was taken aback. "You let them stay the night? That's... kind of you," she said softly.

Yoyo smiled. Shelia lingered by the door. It was very late now, and Shelia was apprehensive about walking home alone even though she lived close by. And she had to ask something. "But... but, wouldn't that turn some people off from visiting here? There's a homeless shelter not too far from here. Why can't they go there?"

Yoyo sighed. "The people who run the shelter, bless their souls, they're angels among us. But homeless shelters ain't too pleasant places. I don't blame these guys for wanting to stay here," she said, pointing with her thumb cocked behind her. "As for scarin' away some customers, I don't want snooty clientele anyway. It's about community, right?" she winked. "Wait here," she added suddenly. Shelia obliged. She came back with a knife. "Here. To keep you safe on your walk back. Walk like you'd damned well use it against any motherfucker who tries to touch you, alright?" she smiled sweetly.

This lady could be someone's grandmother. She took the knife, a little in awe. *Was* she a grandmother? Shelia would ask her sometime.

"Bye," Shelia said, closing the door behind her. Shelia thought about Yoyo's advice as she walked home, streetlights guiding her in the inky night. Was it possible that she'd absorbed people's desires for herself and believed they were her own this whole time?

Since the lay-off announcement, the atmosphere at Cogville had taken a decidedly worse turn. There was an undercurrent of fear. However, the most prevalent thing was denial. Most people pushed the possibility of being laid off to the back of their minds, carrying on their duties as normal. Shelia was a bit of an oddity in regards to this, as well as Olivia, who always asked if people were OK. Even Shelia.

"Um. Yeah. Thanks," she said, surprised. Shelia wanted to continue on, talk about how Olivia was right about the fish store. But what would she say? *Hi Olivia, I went to a fish store, and it was cool?* Shelia decided to say nothing.

Later, she realized Olivia wouldn't care if Shelia sounded like a simpleton. She would just be happy Shelia was expressing something honest; positive. And like, not being a bitch for once.

Maybe I'll tell her some other time. Shelia knew she probably wouldn't, though.

Shelia had hardly interacted with her coworkers since that fateful meeting. She normally kept to herself, anyway, exchanging pleasantries when needed; or occasionally going for drinks, but this time, everyone else kept to themselves too. Or maybe they just kept away from her. Normally someone would swing by her cubicle to say their words of the day. Shelia had never done the same for any of her coworkers. If they hadn't behaved like respectable sociable people, Shelia would have been more of a loner than she already was.

The end was nigh, and Shelia felt strangely nostalgic. She felt like she could maybe attempt to join the ranks of normal, nice people.

"Hey, Jeremiah," Shelia said, waving slightly, just outside his cubicle entrance. He swivelled his chair towards her, surprised. She awkwardly ambled into the space.

"Hey," he said. "What's up?"

"Oh, you know, just seeing what's up with you."

Jeremiah nodded along, pretending this was a normal occurrence. But then he stopped pretending. "You don't usually do that," he chuckled.

Damn. Why did he have to go and be honest about things? What could Shelia reply to this — *Yeah, I didn't because I'm an antisocial freak?* She scrambled her brains.

"Well, you know how you said you and Elizabeth were working on a new program and were going to show it next meeting, but then you know, last meeting happened and it wasn't really a great time?"

Jeremiah was intrigued, and waited for her to continue. Shelia stopped. *Where am I going with this again?* "Um. Yeah, so I was wondering if you'd show it to me. I could've stopped by Elizabeth's, but your cubicle was closer, so…" she trailed off. "Yeah."

Jeremiah's face lit up. "Glad you asked," he said, smiling. He popped his head over the cubicle wall and called out, "Yo,

Elizabeth! Shelia wants to check out our program. Wanna come over?"

"Sure," she called out. Jeremiah opened up the application. "Basically, what we did was take this entire middle section of the old code—"

"And we completely overhauled it. Mostly by combining a lot of functions into one," Elizabeth added behind them, putting her hand on Jeremiah's shoulder.

"Yeah. And what this does is it streamlines the process dramatically. Before, whenever an operation needed to be done it took about two seconds. Now, it's about 0.5," Jeremiah said.

"And that adds up to saving about an hour for every average use of the program," Elizabeth concluded.
Shelia looked the new code over. It was sleek, innovative; basically a work of art. It reminded her of why she loved coding in the first place.

"Wow. I mean, this is amazing," Shelia said. "Have you showed it to the boss? This... You'd have to be an idiot to lay you guys off after this, that's for sure," she smirked.
Jeremiah and Elizabeth smiled appreciatively, partly because Shelia could joke about lay-offs. It was almost blasphemy, but it cut the sense of doom down to size.

"We did," Elizabeth started hesitatingly, "but nothing came of it, in the end."

"With the finished product, we ended up not using any of the new code because it didn't exactly fit with the contractor's outline," Jeremiah elaborated.

"Even though it's clearly better."

Jeremiah exhaled. "Bureaucracy, I tell you."

Yeah, that sounds about right. "Of course," she said, rolling her eyes. She softened. "You guys should be proud of yourselves anyway. It's great work."

"Thanks, Shelia. That means a lot, coming from you."

Surprised, Shelia responded with a smile.

When she got back to her cubicle, she noticed the phone was ringing. She picked it up. "Hi," said Steve, "Can you come to the main office?" Her heart was pounding. *Was this it? Was this the end?* She almost wanted to ask if they were going to lay her off now, get it over with. Why didn't they just do that instead of inducing anxiety by stringing people along? The walk to the office felt infinite.

She took a breath, and walked in. Shelia sat down, nervously tapping her fingers. "Okay, so... I'm fired, right?" she blurted out.

Steve looked up from his screen. "What?" he laughed incredulously. "No. We think you're one of the best programmers here. I actually wanted your input for this problem. It crashes when the program comes up to this point," he said, pointing at the trouble area.

Shelia blinked. *Not fired, huh...* She looked through the code carefully.

When she was done, she concluded, "You should add another pathway for the condition of a skewed distribution."

Steve looked back at the code. His face lit up. He quickly typed some new code in, and ran the program again. After it ran through, he said, "Works perfectly. Shelia, you're brilliant."

Shelia sat there for a bit. This was the point where she should naturally leave and go back to her duties, but a nagging feeling made her stay. "If I'm so brilliant..." she started, hesitatingly, "how come I didn't get promoted?"

Steve's smile vanished. He cleared his throat. "Well, you're a great computer person, that's for sure, but Olivia is a great people person. You're perfect where you're at."

Shelia chewed on this. She could leave it at that. Or she could stick up for herself a bit. With great effort, she started, "I do agree that Olivia is very charismatic. However, I still believe I would have done great at the new position, given the chance."

Steve nodded. He said, diplomatically, "Next time we're in the position to promote people, I will definitely consider you,"

"Alright. Thank-you," she said. When she walked out, she thought, in disbelief, *I still have my damn job.* What she dreaded ultimately did not come to pass. She felt strangely disappointed it hadn't.

The next day, Shelia tapped away on some incredibly boring software, dragging herself through each line of code. function = |, she typed. *What the hell was the function again?* Instinctively, she opened up Monkey Quest. She then closed it immediately, annoyed with herself. *Why am I doing this?* As in, why was she playing Monkey Quest, and why was she still where was she seemingly always was: sitting in her cubicle, hating everything?

Her mind recalled Jeremiah and Elizabeth's beautiful interface. She looked back to the clunky code she was currently working on. Without thinking, she started tweaking it maniacally. When she glanced at the time, an hour had passed. She surveyed the new code, feeling satisfied. That feeling dissipated when she realized Steve would only ask her to undo everything she just did. *"Doesn't comply with our model,"* he'd say simply.

Yoyo's words echoed through her head. *"If I were you, I'd just quit instead of waiting for the ball to drop."* Well, the ball didn't drop (on her), *but maybe...* she thought scandalously, *I should quit anyway.* The thought filled her with excitement.

Her pragmatic side quickly shut that down. *No. If I quit, I should have another job lined up.* She sighed. She opened up Monkey Quest again. Instead of mindlessly playing it, she decided to analyze its code.

Oh. So that's how they get the monkey to do its twisty-tail thing, she smiled.

"Playing Monkey Quest again?" Mark smirked behind her, startling Shelia.

She turned her head. "I'm, in fact, not playing it, but looking at its code," she said haughtily.

Mark took a closer look. "Man, being a video game developer. That'd be the life," he said wistfully. "What're you working on there?"

"Just some work for the contractor," she said. "I edited it... but, Steve will just ask me to undo it," she said regretfully. She had to force her fingers to go over the 'Control' and 'Z' buttons.

"Hold on there," he said. "Why don't you just show him anyway?"

"Jeremiah and Elizabeth did something similar, and they got shut down," she said.

"Well. Maybe he won't shut you down," Mark said, clapping her on the shoulder. "Consider it," he said as he left her cubicle.

She looked at her edited masterpiece. She regarded it like a baby. *Okay, I have to at least try to save this thing.*

"Doesn't comply with our model," Steve said, after hearing Shelia's spiel. Shelia sat there, deflated. *Goddamnit. Why did I get my hopes up?*

"I don't get it. You have to agree that this is more optimal than the original. Why don't we just ask the client if they like this version better, complying with model or not?"

Steve rubbed his forehead. "First Jeremiah and Elizabeth, now you," he said. "I don't get why you people don't understand that my models are here for a reason."

Shelia was alarmed at his sudden irritation, but she didn't backtrack. "Alright," she said gently, "May I know the reasoning behind them?"

"No," he said simply. Steve sighed. "Look, all I want is for you guys to follow instructions. It's not that hard."

Shelia clenched her fists. *Alright, that's fucking it.* She took a breath so she could avoiding outright yelling.

"Steve, with all due respect, I think you're making a mistake by ignoring your employees' innovations," she said tightly. "I... can't work in this kind of environment, one that suppresses creativity, anymore. I have to resign," she said.

Steve looked incredulous. "Quitting, in this economy?" he said. "Good luck finding another job," he snorted.

Shelia tapped her fingers. "I can still get a recommendation from you, right?"

"Yeah, yeah. You deserve that much, after all the troubleshooting you've done for me," he said grudgingly.

"Alright. You can call me up for advice anytime. But, you'll have to pay me... as a consultant," she said, coming up with the idea on the spot. She was faking her bravado. Advocating for herself in such a way was a foreign thing to her, and she felt nervous.

Steve nodded. "Since you're not technically laid off, I'm not giving you a severance package."

Shelia exhaled. "Great. Okay," she said, sarcasm just peeking through. She stood up.

"We'll sort through the paperwork later," he said definitively.

She walked back from Steve's office in a daze. She just stood in the centre of all the cubicles, a bit numb. Passersby looked at her curiously. *Wait, I guess I didn't do the two-weeks-notice- thing.* But neither she nor Steve seemed to have cared about that formality. *So... I guess I should start packing?*

"Hi guys," she called out, to nobody and everybody. "So... I just quit. I'm sorry for sometimes being an asshole. You're all great," she said with finality. She commenced packing.
A few seconds later, Mark was at her cubicle. "Shelia, what the actual fuck? I told you to show your code to Steve, and then you end up quitting?"

"Yeah. I guess."

"If you're lucky enough to have a job in this economy, you keep it!" he said, crossing his arms.

"Dude, don't rain on her parade. Can't you see how excited she is?" Jeremiah said, popping up beside Mark. By chance, she caught her reflection in the monitor at that moment. She had to admit she looked less mournful than usual.

Soon, Elizabeth, Olivia, and Lily showed up. "Sometimes being an asshole? Try all the time," Lily said, without a trace of irony.

Shelia shrugged and said, "That's fair." Lily was taken aback by her easy admission.

Shelia turned to Lily. She opened her mouth, and then closed it again. "Lily... there's a reason you're here, even though you're so young. You've... got stuff, okay?" Shelia said, with difficulty.

Lily became even more surprised. The statement, by itself, was not that heartwarming, but coming from Shelia, it was akin to a declaration of love. Lily lit up and hug-attacked Shelia. To Shelia's further alarm, Olivia, Jeremiah, and Elizabeth soon followed.

"Mark, don't be such a wet rag. Join in!" Jeremiah said.

"Yeah, c'mon Mark," Olivia teased.

Mark grumbled, but he caved. Thus, Shelia found herself in the middle of five humans attempting to squeeze her. *I did not sign up for this,* she thought, as her life-force slowly ebbed away. But she smiled nonetheless.

After the obligatory paperwork was signed, and her cubicle had been emptied, Shelia and Steve shook hands.

"Take care, Shelia," Steve said.

"You too," she said. Even though Steve was rather authoritarian, she'd appreciated that he never underestimated her abilities, as she commonly experienced as a woman in a male-dominated industry.

Still, she could have added, *Nice working here,* but she felt impervious to false pleasantries, at the moment.

Olivia caught her on her final way out the door.

"Hey, Shelia," she said softly. "I'm really proud of you. You're finally doing what's true to you."

Is that what I'm doing, now? This thought forced Shelia to confront the reality of her actions. There was no going back. Shelia shrugged in response. Olivia placed her hand on her shoulder. "Don't worry too much. You'll figure something out. Leap, and the net will appear, right?"

I always thought only idiots did that. Now, I guess, I've become one of those idiots. Shelia exhaled. "I'm actually... not so sure of that, Olivia," Shelia said honestly.

Olivia nodded. "I understand. You're welcome to come to my networking events, alright? I'll keep you in touch," she said.

"Thanks, Olivia," Shelia said.

Say the thing about the fish. Say something about the fish, Shelia urged herself. Shelia didn't know why this thought nagged her. Maybe because it would be her way of saying, *Sorry. I was wrong about you.*

Well, I mean, I probably was. I'm not sure, because I never gave you a chance.

"Okay. So I'll see you around. Take care, Shelia," Olivia said warmly.

"You too," she said gently. Shelia shut the familiar metal doors behind her, a walking swirl of jumbled feelings.

Oh my God. I'm free. I'm fucking free. She felt giddy as she faced the concrete world outside. She felt like doing a little dance, but refrained. She channeled her energy into enthusiastic walking instead.

But where am I going? Slowly, the practicalities of everything came to her, bringing her back down to earth. She didn't feel ready to settle into her apartment.

"I can't tell whether I prefer 2 am Yoyo's or normal-hours Yoyo's," Shelia said as she came in.

"You've got to be crazy to not pick 2 am," Yoyo said, raising her eyebrow. "So. What can I do ya for today?"

Shelia tapped her fingers on the counter. "Um. I just quit my job?"

"You sound like you're not sure if you quit your job or not."

"Okay. I quit my job."

Yoyo looked at her, waiting for her to go on. Shelia wasn't planning on saying anything else, but Yoyo's stare seemed to coax words out of her.

"I'm happy about it but... I'm not sure what to do with myself," Shelia said quietly.

Yoyo nodded. She took slow steps out from behind the counter, and headed towards the back of the store. Shelia followed. Yoyo pointed to a pile of boxes in the corner.

"This box goes in the romance section, that one is comics, this one is mystery... Standard alphabetical order. Think you can handle it?"

"Um, yeah." From where she was standing, she could see the table-area she sat in the last time she visited. This time, there were youths occupying the area; the collective look an assortment of baggy pants, cleavage, fat baseball caps, heavy make-up, and skater shoes. They were either reading, playing chess, or talking loudly.

"They look like gangsters," Shelia commented.

Yoyo rolled her eyes. "Society's the real gangster."

If for nothing else, the unpaid labour was worth it for the comedic value of the romance section. Shelia had a good snort at the expense of titles like *Stormy Tempest* and *Sensual Cowboys*.

"Hey, don't knock it 'til ya try it," Yoyo chuckled. "Besides, with your 'failed love life', as you say, it might be a good substitute."

"Maybe you're right," Shelia mused. She finished with the romance section and moved on to mystery. "Yoyo. I've been meaning to ask you. Do you have like, kids, or a husband, or something?"

Yoyo sighed as she shuffled some books on a mostly-empty shelf. "It's a sad story, kid. Maybe another time."

Shelia nodded, quiet. *Damn. Yoyo's so mysterious.* They stacked their books in silence.

"Why does that section have barely any books?" Shelia asked after a while.

"I'm in the process of building it up. It's LGBT."

"Got it."

In due time, the boxes were empty. Yoyo raised her eyebrows at Shelia. "If I were you, I'da been out celebrating the end of a shitty job with some girlfriends instead of stackin' books."

Celebrating with some girlfriends. Shelia paused. *What a novel concept.* She hadn't done such a thing since she left Waterloo. Yoyo scrutinized Shelia's face, and then burst out laughing. "Don't tell me your friend situation is in the pits, too." Shelia couldn't help but smile. She appreciated Yoyo's light approach to things that felt daunting.

"Okay. My default social interaction would be going for drinks with my coworkers. The thing is, I don't—well, I didn't —like them, at all. But then I started liking them recently." Shelia puzzled over her situation. "And then... I quit." She looked at Yoyo. "Did I just fuck everything up?"

"Definitely a possibility," Yoyo said. Shelia nodded.

"You really have no friends outside of work?"
Shelia shook her head.

"Well," Yoyo huffed, amused. "Now you're in a sink-or-swim situation. Start putting yourself out there," Yoyo said, clapping her on the back.

Shelia had never "put herself out there" in her life. She'd had the same group of nerdy girlfriends she met in advanced classes from junior high to post-university. She'd passively gone from one built-in social group (school friends) to another (work friends), pretty much unconsciously, Shelia was realizing.

"I'll try. I guess," Shelia said.

"Atta girl."

Just as Shelia was about to shut the door behind her, Yoyo said, "Wait."

"What?" Shelia asked, her head peeking through the mostly-closed door.

"I still don't know your goddamn name," Yoyo said amusedly.

"Oh. Shit," Shelia laughed. "It's Shelia."

It was the middle of the week, and she was at her house at 2 pm. Which made her alternate between feeling exhilarated, guilty, and subversive. *Either way, getting to sleep in on a Wednesday is pretty awesome.*

She slouched into her old suede couch. Weirdly enough, she didn't feel like watching TV or anything of the sort. It was like she'd been using entertainment to distract and uplift herself from her reality, and now that she didn't have anything she wanted to be distracted from, she didn't know what to do.

Indefinite limbo confronted her. *Actually,* Shelia thought. *I have a maximum of four months of this no-agenda thing. If I don't find another job by then…* Shelia tilted her head back into her couch. *I guess I'll have do a LOT of downsizing.*

Technically, she'd always earned a lot of money in her professional life, and collected a decent amount of savings because she'd always thought of herself as a Financially Responsible Person—until now.

Now, she had to re-evaluate her lifestyle. Constant drinks with the coworkers she didn't relate to, always eating out because

she was always too tired to cook, the rent on her modern apartment, the monthly payments on her nice car...
The financial security she achieved, and all of the trappings that came with it, were a point of pride for her, and now all of it coming into question.
What if I downsize and am still screwed? Does that mean I have to move back in with my parents? She frowned at the thought.
She was caught off-guard when her cell rang. It was, coincidentally, her parents' number.

"Hiiiiii," Shelia said. Her casual countenance changed when she realized she'd actually have to tell her parents that she was currently jobless and had nothing lined up. She could only imagine their reaction. *Alright. I am so not doing that right now.*

"Shi-lei. Have you contacted Dipon yet?" her mom asked in Chinese.
Shelia was used to her mother's tendency to get straight to the point, but without context Shelia was lost for the moment. "Um. Who?"

"Dipon. John's friend."
Oh. That scatterbrained blind date that my family is trying to set me up on. "No," she said flatly.

"Okay. I've just contacted him for you. Let's see..." she paused for a moment. Shelia took this moment to get her bearings on what was happening.

"Wait, what? Why would you—"

"He has replied, and has agreed to meet you Wednesday at 6'o clock at Rosemary's Tea," she said, cutting Shelia off.

"What…" Shelia slapped her hand to her face. "I did not ask you to do this," Shelia said sternly. "Just tell him I can't make it." She added, "And then never set me up on any more random dates again."

"Shi-lei, don't sadden this man," her mom said. "I've done this for your own good. Here, talk to Dad."

"What? Ma—"

"Shi-lei, listen to your mother," her dad said. "And how are you?"

"Tell Ma I have not agreed!" Shelia said indignantly. "And I'm fine. How are you?"

"Good."

"That's good to hear."

This was usually the extent of her and her father's conversations. After the brief silence, her dad said, "Okay. I'll hang up now. Talk to you soon," like clockwork.

"Bye," she said, hanging up. Shelia was glad that her job didn't come up in conversation because it meant she didn't have to lie about not having one.

The next time Shelia came in to Yoyo's, she was tasked with the Science Fiction section.

"So, you're just going to be here more often because you have nothing better to do?" Yoyo asked.

"Okay… I guess that's like a thank-you for the free labour I am providing," Shelia smirked.

"Hey girly, what about the free advice *I'm* providing?"

"Touché."

The crowd at the hidden table area was similar to the one that was there the last time Shelia had visited. One of the teenagers came up and approached Yoyo. Shelia felt her guard come up at the sight of him: he was big and intimidating-looking in black, baggy clothes.

"Hey Yoyo. Our set is missing a bishop. Do you have any extras?" he asked, gesturing to the elaborately-set chess game behind him, where a similarly-dressed teenager was sitting. Shelia was surprised at how soft-spoken he was.

"Hmm," Yoyo said. She hobbled to her desk and pulled out a small object from the drawer. "You could use this," she said, placing it in the teenager's hand. It was a small, intricately painted turtle. He surveyed it, smiling faintly. His smile faded when he noticed Shelia regarding his and Yoyo's interaction. Shelia quickly looked away and stuffed 'Escape from Yewtia' in between two random sci-fi novels.

"Whats up with her? She doesn't look Native."

"Hell. Even lots of Natives don't look Native," Yoyo mused.

"Why is she here?" he asked, in a curious, rather than accusatory, tone.

"Ask her herself. She won't bite," Yoyo smiled, raising her eyebrow.

He hesitatingly looked at Shelia. He figured he didn't have to repeat the question.

Shelia felt put on the spot. "Right. Um. I'm here because I don't know what else to do."

He considered her predicament. "Just do what you gotta do," he shrugged.

"What if this is what I have to do?" she wondered aloud.

"That's unlikely," he said.

"Well, now," Yoyo smiled, "Not everything in life is so linear, Justin. Sometimes the things you need at the moment come from some really random shit."

"Ohh. I see," Justin said thoughtfully.

"But you could be right. Shelia might be completely wasting her time right now!" Yoyo cackled. Justin laughed, and headed back to the hidden table area. "Thanks for the turtle," he called out.

"She's a turtle-bishop now," Yoyo said solemnly.

Shelia leafed through a random book. "You know," she said, "I don't feel like I am. Wasting my time, that is. But I agree with Justin, intellectually."

Yoyo considered her. "I think you don't feel like you're wasting your time precisely because you're 'wasting your time.'"

Shelia paused her leafing. "Huh?"

"You're the kinda person who's went from Point A to Point B all 'er life. Right now, all ya have to do is be. This expanse of time staring you square in the face probably freaks the hell out of ya, but it's exactly what you need… To sit with your goddamn self without all these distractions."

"But… don't you think it's a little impractical to spend too much time 'just sitting with your goddamn self'? That seems like wasting time. There are things to be done, responsibilities to take care of…"

Yoyo rolled her eyes. "Nobody's asking you to make like Buddha and sit under a tree for a year. Or however long it was," Yoyo said with a wave of her hand. "In fact, you're gonna have to hustle to make it," Yoyo said. "But to make sure you're hustling at the right things, you gotta get to know yourself. Loosen your grip, and let things unfold. Then it'll be hustling without the struggle. You've been living without taking time to just be all your life, and look at where that's got ya."

Shelia took in her words. She didn't want to be able to recognize herself in Yoyo's description, but she did. *How the hell can she read into my life like it's one of these books over here?*

"Hey, but I'm here right now. That's not exactly going from "Point A to Point B", is it?"

"You're right," Yoyo allowed. "But you better make sure ya don't use this to replace your old habits and avoid dealing with yourself. It can be helpful to have something to anchor yourself against a sea of nothingness, but sometimes, ya just gotta float with the nothingness."

Shelia nodded slowly. She wasn't sure if what Yoyo was saying was magical hoo-ha, but it didn't seem like it.

"How are you so damn wise?" Shelia asked.

"Mystical Indian Powers," Yoyo said dryly. "And I'm also old," she said, smirking.

3

Resumé. |, Shelia typed. She sat at her laptop and stared at the screen for five minutes. *Right. Next section is…education.* She pressed 'enter' twice. Bachelor of Engineering, University of Waterloo, she typed. She moved on to the skills section. Before her degree, bullshit filler words like 'hardworking' and 'efficient' would have gone in that section. Now, Shelia could use actual shit like 'Proficient in Javascript and C++'.

She finished the thing, and then sent it to five companies she'd found via classifieds. *Damn. I'm so productive,* Shelia thought, satisfied with herself.

Shelia absently picked off a paint-chip from the white chocolate bar door.

"Hey Yoyo, you should get your door repainted," Shelia said when she came in. Yoyo was in the middle of bringing the teens some tea. When they saw her, they started pointing and talking.

"It's that Asian chick," Justin said to his friend.

"Shelia," she muttered. "My name is Shelia…"

Yoyo chuckled, and turned to Shelia again. "I don't have any books for you to stack today. You could paint the door if you wanted," she shrugged.

Painting, huh? A change of pace. "Yoyo, I was wondering. Am I the only non-native patron of this place?"

Yoyo walked back to the counter and slowly plopped herself onto her chair. "My customers are pretty mixed, but you're one of the handful of non-native regulars," she said. "And the only Asian one."

"Got it." Shelia glanced back at the table area, filled with people who couldn't legally drink yet. *At 2 am we've got homeless old dudes, and now, we've got the tween crowd.* "Shouldn't they be in school right now?"

"Should is subjective," Yoyo said simply.

Shelia was mildly scandalized. "You're encouraging skipping class to impressionable children?"

"I encourage learning," Yoyo corrected. "Monica! What class ya skipping this time?" she hollered over to the back.

"Chemistry," Monica called out.

Yoyo nodded. She scribbled something onto a post-it note and then passed it to Shelia. "Can you get this book and give it to Monica? It's in YA."

"Um, sure." The book in question was 'The Sweetness at the Bottom of the Pie'. Shelia retrieved it and then headed into the tween turf.

"Here," she said, giving it to the girl named Monica. She was skinny, (Shelia guessed she was about fourteen), and she had make-up game that rivalled a grown woman's. "I guess Yoyo thinks you'll like it."

Monica flipped the book over once or twice. "Alright." Done with scrutinizing the book, she scrutinized Shelia, looking her up and down. "Hey. You're kind of pretty. What's up with you, anyway?"

Shelia was a bit taken aback by being called pretty. It didn't happen much. Before Shelia could respond, Justin turned from his chess game and said, matter-of-factly, "She doesn't know what to do with her life."

"No. I mean, what's really up with you? Like, do you have a boyfriend or are you married or something? What kind of job do you have?"

"Um, alright," Shelia said, deciding to take on the questions. She noticed that it wasn't just Monica and Justin listening to her anymore. "No boyfriend, not married, and... no job."

"Ouch," she said, raising her eyebrows. The eavesdroppers had similar looks of sympathy.

Shelia laughed self-deprecatingly. "Yeah, so... you can see why I'm at this stage. I did used to be a programmer. Technically, a software engineer. I quit a week ago."

"What did you do there?"

"Ummm..." Shelia racked her brains for how to explain what she did, exactly. "Well, I can show you. Yoyo, can I borrow your computer?" Shelia called out.

"Have at 'er!" Yoyo replied.

"I'm gonna check it out, too," Justin said. A few other people got up with Monica and Justin as well, following Shelia to the front desk. With a few clicks on Yoyo's computer, Shelia pulled up the source code of Monkey Quest. Justin brightened up when he spotted it. "Hey, I play that sometimes!" he said.

"Me too," said a girl whose name Shelia didn't know yet.

"Yeah?" Shelia said. "Well, at my job, I basically played around with this same kind of language that Monkey Quest uses. Except I used it to make more boring things like statistical models and such."

"It looks like mumbo jumbo," Monica laughed. "But it's cool how that mumbo jumbo can turn into Monkey Quest."

"Yeah. It is," Shelia smiled.

The teens ambled back to their corner. Shelia was surprised to see that Monica actually started reading the book.

"So… Why did you give her 'Sweetness at the Bottom of the Pie', anyway?" Shelia asked Yoyo.

"The main character, a young girl, uses chemistry to solve murder mysteries. I figured it might help pique Monica's interest in her studies."

"Wow. Sneaky." Shelia said. At that moment, a cluster of vibrations attacked Shelia's hip, making her jump a little. After a second of cognitive dissonance Shelia realized it was her phone, and she'd just received a text. *What a freakin' novelty,* she thought, pulling her cell from her pocket. The text was from an unrecognized number.

Hi Shelia, it's Dipon. John's friend, AKA that random-ass guy that your mom is trying to set you up with. Which I know is kind of weird. I thought it might be interesting just because it was so weird.
What do you think? Can you make it to Rosemary's, Wednesday at six?

Best,
Dipon

Shelia skimmed the message, not quite sure what to think of this Dipon character. *Okay, so, he's self-aware.* But she didn't like the idea of someone going out with her for the heck of it. *And who formats a text like an email, anyway?* She typed No thanks but didn't send it, because she didn't like responding to texts immediately. (When she got them, at least).

"Who was that?" Yoyo asked absently, wiping her glasses with her sleeve.

"Oh, jeez. Just some guy that my mom is trying to set me up with. It's so weird," Shelia said, shaking her head. Monica came up behind Shelia and slid 'The Secret at the Bottom of the Pie' forward. "Thanks for the book, Yoyo. I'm gonna go off to art class now," she said. She turned to Shelia and said, "You should go out with the guy, and then make fun of him with your girlfriends if you have a sucky time!"

"Ha. Thanks for the tip," Shelia said. She wouldn't go into the fact that she didn't have girlfriends with this random fourteen year-old just yet. Shelia waved to Monica on her way out, the bell tinkling behind her.

"Maybe you should let yourself be set up. Y'know, expand your social circle beyond teenagers and old bookkeepers."

"But, Yoyo," Shelia said, fluttering her eyes profusely, "You're all I need!"

Yoyo stared at her for a second before snorting.

Jest aside, Shelia could see the Yoyo's point. She slowly considered changing her mind. *It wouldn't technically hurt,* she thought cautiously. *And if it does go badly, well. At least I can make fun of of him with my girlfriends.*

Thus, as Shelia mulled over her dismal social network on her walk home, No thanks turned into: Ok. see you then.

The tea place was located in a hip millennial neighbourhood, and as such, had non-existent parking. Shelia found a spot about five blocks away, and powerwalked to Rosemary's, passing by vintage boutiques, record stores, and weed shops. She smoothed her dress—not too fancy, not too casual—before walking into the sea of pink that was Rosemary's.

The question of how good she wanted to look had been a serious mental dilemma. On one hand, the ego-boost of appearing to be in a higher 'league' than her date was tempting. But on the other, she didn't want to convey the idea that she was terribly invested in the whole thing. *I mean, I'm not even attracted to brown guys.* So she went for the safe, middle-of-the-road approach.

Dipon spotted her, and waved. Shelia was caught off-guard by his mix of delicate and strong features. *Huh. He's not bad-looking.* His being better-looking than she expected did not, however, change her apathy for how the date would go. *If I don't care about this date so much, then why am I even going? Right. To 'put myself out there' and 'expand my social circle'. Or be spontaneous, or whatever.*

"Hey," she said, sitting down. "Sorry I'm late. Parking is—"

"Crazy. Yeah. I probably should have warned you," he said, smiling.

The subsequent millisecond of pause had Shelia inwardly panicking. *Oh, shit. Is there going to an awkward silence now? Are we going to launch into inane small talk to avoid it?*

"I'm glad you didn't invite me to dinner," she said suddenly. Dipon blinked, surprised at her hastiness. Then he nodded. "Tea, or coffee, is enough time to know whether you like someone. No need to painstakingly go through a three-course meal with someone you don't click with."

"Huh. Yeah. I guess there's that, too." Shelia said. "But also… it's so… so ritualized, I guess."

"Interesting. I didn't consider that. With the right company, though, it's not too bad," he said good-naturedly.

"Yeah, I guess so," Shelia said, conceding his point. *When was the last time I had a good time at dinner, with good people?*

A waitress with a buzz cut came over with Dipon's tea. "Excellent. Thank-you," he said.

"Anything for you?" she asked Shelia.

"Uh. I'll have the oolong."

Dipon took a sip of his matcha. "I'm glad you agreed to come. I wasn't expecting you to."

Shelia played with an errant string on the hem of her dress. "I wasn't going to. But here, apparently, I am," she shrugged.

"So..." he asked, "What changed your mind?"

Shelia sighed. "Having a shitty social life."

"So you didn't come for romantic reasons?" he asked.

Shelia shook her head. "I mean, I'm supposed to have..." she trailed off.

"No, thats all good," he said quickly. "I was waiting to tell you this, but I'm not, either. When John set us up, I was single at the time. But now, I've started going steady with a guy. I agreed to come because I love meeting new people. And... because your mom sounded so excited about the prospect of a date," he added.

Shelia groaned, putting her hand to her face. "I still can't believe my mom would butt into my life like this. It's so embarrassing."

Dipon looked at her sympathetically. "I can see your point. It's sweet that she cares about you so much, though."

"I think it's more that she doesn't want to be associated with having a spinster daughter. But, sure, it could be concern for my well-being," she said dryly.

They both sipped their tea at the same time: the slurping noise, eerily synchronized.

"This would be, like, really shitty if I was here looking for romance, though," she laughed.

"Um… yeah. I'm glad it worked out and that we're on the same page, though."

Shelia nodded. Seconds rolled by, and neither Dipon or Shelia had any ready words to offer. She was finished her tea and had nothing to busy herself with. She panicked, and struggled through a list of things she could say. *I could question him about pets? Or the… economy?*

"So, what do you like to do for fun?" he asked warmly. Shelia frowned. *So this is what we're gonna talk about?*

"Nothing," she said, matter-of-factly. She had an inkling that wasn't true, but she didn't feel like thinking hard about what she actually liked to do.

Dipon blinked at her. "I doubt that. I mean… you don't read books? Watch sports? Volunteer?" he tried.

Shelia thought about the last book she "read". For some reason, she didn't feel like advertising the fact that she'd been reading 'A Practical Guide to Life'.

"Not really," she said. She realized it would be the epitome of social failure if she left it at that. Thus, she added, "What… about you?"

"Well," he started. "I'm super into fitness. I jog 10 miles a day. I hike whenever I can. And I love traveling. Since I'm an accountant, and I can find a job for that anywhere, I live in a new area every two years or so. Before here, I was in Bermuda."

"Wow. You're super interesting."

"Um…" Dipon looked at her quizzically, trying to read her tone. "Are you being sarcastic?"

"No, I'm not."

"Alright then. I guess you're just one of those people who sound sarcastic by default," he said, sighing.

"I guess so."

Another silence. "You know… you're an interesting person. Witty. But, you're pretty boring on paper."

Shelia took a second to process that Dipon was moving from polite discourse onto light criticism of character. She crossed her arms. "Gee, thanks for your input. I'll make sure to become interesting *on paper* as well so I'm suitable to have tea with next time," she said, the sarcasm dripping from her tongue.

"I don't mean it in a harsh way. You know, I used to not look people in the eye, until a random person pointed it out to me? I just think that social pointers can be helpful."

Shelia stared at him. "So, what? I'm like a charity project?"

He replied, calmly, "I just want to help."

Shelia shook her head in disbelief. "Okay, well. This date has devolved from an actual date to a friend date, and now, even that has failed. Goodbye," she said, getting up.

"What, you're leaving?" he said incredulously. "Friends don't let other friends live blindly to their flaws," he called out, as she left the sea of pink.

You're boring, she thought, staring at the ceiling. Since quitting her job two weeks ago, she'd gotten into a steady routine of sleeping in, applying to jobs, and then heading to Yoyo's. However, today, she'd spent the morning binge-watching *Vengeful Mamas.*

She lay on the couch, laptop and an empty bag of chips pushed aside. *You're an asshole. You're friendless. Jobless. And relationship-less.* She shut her eyes. *Just less-than, in general.* She opened her eyes. They landed on the empty bag of chips. Shelia looked at it scornfully. *Stop being a lazy piece of shit, and do something productive,* she willed herself angrily. She got up, her muscles dragging through the air as if it were gravel.

She flipped open her laptop flippantly, and checked her inbox. She'd applied for about forty jobs via classifieds, and she had ten responses in return. All of them said something like, 'We are currently processing your application. Due to an overwhelming number of submissions, only successful applicants will be contacted.'

I'm very qualified, she thought grumpily. She sighed. *I should apply for more jobs.* She pulled up a job classifieds site, and clicked on one stating, 'Seeking Developer'. She stared at the screen for five minutes. *Wow. I really don't feel like doing this.* She shut her laptop.

Look at you. You're pathetic. You're almost thirty, and you don't know what you're doing with your life.

Out of the corner of her eye, she spotted something abominable. She started laughing spitefully: it was *A Practical Guide to Life*. Gathering dust on the corner of her coffee table. *Alright, universe, you're playing a joke on me.* She grabbed the book. *Well, I'm in on it.* She flipped through pages forcefully, and landed on a random one.

STOP BEING AN ASSHOLE (TO YOURSELF)

'Would you stay friends with someone who behaved the way you do to yourself?

How do you even know how you behave with yourself, anyway?

The first thing you can do is take stock of your thoughts. When you think of yourself, are your thoughts more like A) I shouldn't have eaten those brownies. I'm a fat, lazy fuck or B) I put a lot of effort into that project. Even if it didn't work out, that counts for something ?

Unless you're an idiot, you can probably tell that having thoughts that are more like "B" indicate a better relationship with yourself. Easier said than done to be less like person A, though.

So, what's the deal, if you're person A right now? Do you think that you're not a person worth liking in the first place? It doesn't matter. Override that idea and commit to liking yourself anyway. Just suspend your goddamn disbelief if you have to, at first.

Not liking yourself actually makes you a worse person, because if you don't like yourself, you have a smaller pool to give to your relationships. In other words, you're a crappier friend, partner, son, daughter, sibling, husband, grandmother, etc.

Even if you are objectively the worst, and you don't care that you could become a crappy person because of your self-dislike (or self-hatred or self-ambivalence, whatever shade the beast is), you should still do it for convenience. Why?

Think about it. Whenever you make a human mistake, if you like yourself, you won't beat yourself up endlessly over it.

Whenever you recognize you're in a bad situation, be it job-wise, relationship-wise, etc., you'll care about yourself enough to be motivated to change it.

Whenever you have an idea to do something, you won't have to go through the whole self-doubt process before you even begin.

In other words, if you like yourself, it creates a certain lack of obstructions. And your life will be a lot more pleasant.

So... how the hell do you start liking yourself?

It's not an overnight process. If you are in a place of self-loathing simply forcing yourself to think positive thoughts is counter-productive. Just start with being aware that you're being a dick to yourself. And, let's be real, probably others as well.

Once you're mindful of how you speak to yourself: gently orient them towards the better. Be diligent about the thoughts you choose, and your self-talk.

Sit with yourself, sans distractions. Get to know yourself. Don't be scared to actually spend some quality time with little ol' you.

You really can go from being your worst enemy to your own best friend.

The relationship you have to yourself is your longest one, so you best make it a great one.'

She finished reading the section. Instead of feeling pissed off, like she expected, she felt intrigued. She still thought the book was cheesy and trite, but it did cause her to wonder if she was indeed being an asshole to herself. If so, should she actually try to stop being an asshole to herself? *Or is this book full of bullshit, as usual?*

Shelia recalled the letter that was in the book. She wondered where it went. After a bit of a cursory search, she found it within the (abhorrent) millimetre layer of dust under her couch. *Shit, I need to vacuum.*

Twenty minutes of vacuuming her apartment later, she blew the dust off the letter and looked it over again. *Hmm. Candace in BC. Two smart kids, a laid-off husband. And a mother in a retirement home all the way here in Ontario.* She imagined that Candace was around her age. Or maybe a bit older, based on the fact that she had young children. Shelia started to envision her life had it taken a Candace-like timeline. *I mean, I guess it would be the life I'd have had if I stayed with Parker... stayed in my job. Shelia touched her belly lightly. Damn, I might be pregnant by now,* she thought, horrified. *Or have toddlers!*

Shelia looked around her bachelorette pad with new appreciation. She was glad she'd made the choices she did, even if they weren't orthodox. Even if they made her life the unsure mess it was now. *It's better than doing something I know I don't want for my life,* she realized. *It's better than a sure mess.* She scanned the envelope, scanning the addresses. She puzzled over why Candace's mom was called Miss Moon. *Why was the letter in the book instead of with Miss Moon, anyway? And why do they even correspond by snail mail in this age of technology?* she puzzled. *I have no use for it... I might as well go drop it off at this Rivercrest retirement home.*

She put the letter in her purse. As she did so, she noticed her cell was blinking within her purse, and pulled it out.

Olivia: Hey Shelia. I hope you've been well, given the circumstances. We've missed you here at the company!

Missed me? Shelia scoffed, as she read the text. *She must be saying that to be polite.* Shelia continued reading.

I have some sad news. A lot of us have been recently laid off. Me and Mark are still around, but the rest of the crew: Lily, Jeremiah, and Elizabeth, as well as others, have been let go.

So, as I said before, I'm hosting a meetup to help each other through these tough economic times. It'll be Thursday at 7, my place (117 street and Bellevue road.) It would be great to see you there!

Shelia wasn't sure what to think of this invite. So she mentally filed it away and resolved to think about it later.

4

A fidgety middle-aged guy stood at the counter of Yoyo's books. "Do you have 'The Lost Empire of Souls and Doom?'" he asked.

"Yep," Yoyo responded.

"'Yammerchuck?'"

"Uh-huh."

"'Uncrap Your Life?'" he added lastly.

Yoyo nodded.

"Great!" he said. Yoyo proceeded to locate the aforementioned books.

Shelia watched the whole interaction, mildly curious. After the man walked out (books in-tow), she asked Yoyo, "So… do you just have your entire inventory memorized?"

"Yep."

Shelia nodded. "That's impressive. But what happens when you're sick?"

"I hardly get sick," Yoyo said, raising an eyebrow.

Shelia rolled her eyes. "Should've known your moral constitution was so strong that it gave you infinite health." She moseyed to the other side of the counter, and poked around the computer.

"You know, I could set up a database here. That way, you don't have to memorize your entire inventory. And you could, like, take a freaking sick day," she muttered.

"Sure, you can install it if you want. I have a master list of all the books that you can use. But keeping things in my head helps keep it sharp," she winked.

"Alright. It's going to take a long time, though, just so you know."

Yoyo poked around and drudged up the master list, and Shelia idly began the process. The silence, punctuated only by clicks and shuffles, made Shelia feel antsy, after a while.

"Where are those kids?" Shelia asked.

"Dunno. They do things other than hang around here."

"Hey, I do other things, too. Like go on failed dates and watch the entire season of Vengeful Mamas. While pondering where I went wrong in life."

Yoyo stopped her book shuffling, and looked at Shelia. "Listen," she called out, "It's okay to be at a shitty time in your life. It happens. We're human. Sometimes, the best we can do, is slowly crawl out of the shit the best we can," she said.

"Right…" Shelia said, broodingly. After a while, she asked, "So… have you had, uh, experience with crawling out of shit?"

Yoyo breathed out forcefully. "Plenty."

Shelia was scared to ask the next question, but she did anyway. "Can you… say more?"

"No," she'll say. And then we'll continue the tradition of me not knowing shit about Yoyo.

Instead, Yoyo looked at her gamely. "Alright," she grunted. "But let's get some tea for ourselves, 'cause this is gonna be a long one."

Shelia nodded quickly. She got some tea started with what was almost excitement.

When the two sat down, tea in hand, Yoyo said, "Y'know, I don't tell much people about my backstory, but I trust you, Shelia."

Shelia nodded again, solemnly.

"I grew up," she started, "knowing the world had no place for me." She took a long, thoughtful sip. "It started with my parents. I didn't understand it at the time, but they were haun'ed people, my mum and dad. When my grandparents were able to come around, they eased the burden a bit… But

overall, my brother and I grew up with ghosts all around us."
She paused, as if recalling her old ghosts again. Ghosts she
had come to terms with.

"When I was eight, the government came for us. My mum
was crying, she didn't want us to go, but the Indian Agent was
threatening them, y'know. We had to board a train east.

"When we got there, there were stern adults everywhere, in
dreary black clothing. Big, brick buildings. I was separated
from my brother, 'cause they had boys and girls schools. It
seemed like I landed on an alien planet—and I was all by
myself.

"Anytime they caught us speakin' our language, they would
beat us with a strap. Not lightly, either, it would *sting*. Called
it the devil's language. I could get by because we spoke a lot
of English at home, so I understood the nuns, but many of
the other kids didn't. They were confused why they were
gettin' beat.

"I was able to explain the situation to 'em in Cree, secretly.
One of the kids I explained to, her name was Beverly." Yoyo
sighed, looking wistful.

"I soon got accustomed to residential school. All the chores,
the constant prayin'. I learned how best to avoid beatings, but
sometimes they were just gonna happen regardless.

"As I got used to school, I realized it wasn't alien at all. It
looked like it, but the culture was eerily familiar. I couldn't
place it at the time.

"What defined residential school for me, was always being hungry. We knew the nuns had nice food they were keepin' from us. Sometimes me and Bev would go steal their food. Sometimes we'd go out to the nearby farm and get some turnips or somethin'," Yoyo smiled to herself. "Stealing food with Bev were some of the most fun times I've had. She was my best friend in the hell of boarding school. A real treasure.

"We reached our breaking point with being beat, being hungry, being called devils. Even though we started to believe 'em, that we were sinners and needed savin'. There was still a small, defian' part of ourselves that knew otherwise.

"We ran. It helped that it was unseasonably warm that year. Me and Bev, we made it to the train station, and then we parted ways. It was a miracle that I made it back home. It was troubled as usual—but at least there was love there. That's what I needed. Even though, after residential school, I felt like a stranger being back home.

"Over dinner one day, my mum revealed to me that she'd gone to the same school I had. '*What?*' I said t' her. '*Why didn't you tell me?*' She told me she didn't want to accept that my siblings and I would hav'ta go through what she went through, what my dad went through.

"Reflecting on that conversation many years later, it finally clicked for me why I'd found boarding school eerily familiar —My parents had been acting just like how the nuns and priests had behaved towards them.

"Anyways, the admin eventually found me, and sent me back. I was severely punished. They'd got Bev back too. I told her, '*Who cares if they beat us? Let's run away again,*'" Yoyo shook her head. "Bev told me she couldn't, that her parents would be put in jail if she came back," she sighed.

"I was torn. I didn't want to leave without her. So I stayed," Yoyo said, sipping her tea. "Sometimes I wonder what would have happened, had I decided to leave, while Bev stayed. We were *damn* lucky that we made it the first time. Would I have froze to death on another run? Would I have been caught again, and beat so bad that I never recovered from it? Or would I have made it for good? These things, I'll never know." Yoyo sighed, pausing at this point in the story. "In our last year, something happened to Bev. The priest—" She stopped, unable to continue.

Tears silently flowed down her cheeks. Shelia put a hand on Yoyo's shoulder, most acutely feeling the weight of the past in that moment.

"It was evil… the act of stealing someone's innocence from them," Yoyo continued after a while, wiping her eyes. "Bev didn't tell me nothin', but I could tell what happened. She wasn't the same after. She became withdrawn and distant. Sometimes I wonder why Bev had to suffer, when I escaped that particular fate myself. I wondered how life could be so random and cruel.

"Finally—finally, after eight years in that hell, we got to leave. I was sixteen. Bev and I lost touch after that.

"When I reached my parents' place after that last year, I found that there was more trouble than usual. It was decided that it would be best to stay with my grandparents.

"That time I stayed with my grandparents was instrumental to my being. It was a real pivotal point in my life. It was the first time I felt safe. The first time I felt supported. An environment that wasn't plagued with burdens from the past. I got to learn the traditional ways that were stolen away from us… It was a blissful time. I just wish my brother could have joined me. And that I could have seen Bev. At least I saw my brother during the summer breaks.

"I was eighteen when my grandparents died. I'd only stayed with them for two years. I didn't think it was a good idea for me to go back to my parents', so I moved to the city, got a job at the restaurant, and got my first space to myself. I felt so lucky to have my own space… it was a sanctuary. It didn't matter that it was falling apart, tiny, and had the occasional rodent.

"I met a fella at the restaurant. Rob. He was a regular. Charming. We clicked well. Things were great in the beginning. I was in love.

"It's like that saying of the frog bein' boiled in water. You're going along in the relationship and then suddenly there's this moment when you realize—it's bad. That moment was when he pushed me down the stairs.

"Before that, it was just a snide comment here, questioning my intent with a male friend there. Then it's 24-7 criticism.

Isolating me from my budding friendships. Questioning my intent with all males I come into any contact with, be they strangers or coworkers. Stalking me at my job. It got to the point where I had to quit.

"When it got to physical violence, it was shocking, but... I was used to bein' beat. Violence was ingrained into my psyche."

"The violent episodes are spaced out with the good times. I knew my grandparents taught me that beatin' wasn't a part of our traditional ways. But things get blurry. You can't view the situation clearly when you're in the thick of it. But, something clear did come through eventually, and that was, sooner or later he was going to kill me if I didn't get out. I had run away before. I just had to do it again, and do it successfully.

"I got in touch with my brother, Dave, to help me. I didn't want to wait until Dave got here, so I told him I'd meet him out of town, then I hitched a ride east. I slept on the streets in the first town I landed in, before I got a hold of my brother. The streets felt safer than my own home at that point.

"On my first night I saw a box of books by the dump. I wasn't the best reader, but those books helped keep my spirits up those nights I spent on the streets.

"I went back and forth between being scared, and being hopeful. When I was hopeful it seemed like while I didn't have anything on paper, I really had everything. There was all this possibility that was now before me. And, well, when I was scared, it was hard to deal with, because I had a good reason to be.

"Eventually, I got a hold of Dave and he came and got me. He was so mad, askin' me why didn't I tell anyone sooner. I don't know if he understood the brainwashing, the control that happens. But still, I was grateful that he came through for me.

"So I stayed with my brother and his girlfriend Mary. Ended up stayin' for a long time. My brother was living on his girlfriend's reserve at the time, an 'Nishinaabe place. I didn't know what was gonna happen in my life then. Looking back on it, I understand that it was a time of great healing for me. I went to sweats and dances, sat with elders, helped out in my community. It recalled the time I spent with my grandparents. That whole time, I was rewiring my psyche that had been molded in trauma. Y'know…like writing a new program for myself, to replace a faulty one. You can get that, eh Shelia?

"One day, I tagged along with Dave and Mary on a trip they took to the city. They wanted to go shoppin' one afternoon, I wasn't much interested, so I stayed and waited at this sandwich shop. Read the newspaper, watched people go by. When this particular person walked in, I swear my heart skipped a beat. I couldn't believe it. It was… Bev.

"'*Yolanda?*' she said. '*What are you doing here?*' I asked her the same thing. She said, '*I live here.*' And she sat down. And then we tried to fill each other in on the past decade or so. We could see already see it in each other's faces, that so much had happened.

"When Dave and Mary came back from shopping, I told them I'd catch up with 'em later. Bev and I spent the rest of the day just walking around the city, talking. We were enchan'ed with each other.

"We said goodbye the next day. But we knew this time it wouldn't be a decade before the next time we saw each other.

"We started visiting each other constantly. She had persevered and grown so much past the pain, like I had—but I could see that heaviness that she was still carryin' around. *'Beverly, you need to let out the past that you've buried deep inside,'* I urged her. But she refused. She had too much shame," Yoyo sighed.

She waited some time before speaking again. "Eventually, Dave and Mary had children. It was my pleasure and honour to help raise Darren, Jalisa, and Rodney.

"In that time, I was also dating around. Even though, on some level, Bev and I knew we were in love with each other— we didn't consciously acknowledge it to ourselves. I was afraid to. It went against everything the nuns had beat into us, and I was still fighting that programming.

"But Bev called it out one day. She asked me, *'What're ya doin' with these duds you're dating?'* Then I asked her the same thing. Ha!

"She was flustered. I could see the moment of realization on her face when she said, *'I suppose… I'm waiting around for*

103

you.' Then it was my turn to be flustered. I was brainwashed into believin' that the man-woman model was the only option available. But at that moment, even though I was very afraid to, I couldn't deny my love for her any more. We held both of our hands aloft, and started our relationship in earnest.

"In the beginning, we both wrestled with if what we were doin' was right. Remembering the old teachings, remembering how it taught that spirits like Bev and I were sacred, helped us find our truth.

"After a while of being *together* together, in what you kids'd call a 'long distance relationship'— Beverly eventually asked me, "Yoyo, why don't you come and live with me?"'"

"I thought about it. I wanted to, but I also knew that I wanted to be there for my brother's family. And Bev respected that.

"So, you know, I helped raise the kids for a decade. I loved raising them, watching them become their own people.

"After they were a bit grown, that choice came up again, internally, about whether I wanted to stay in the place that was now home, the place where I had found myself—or follow the winds of change.

"I sat on the choice for a while, until that inner whisper became a shout. I asked Bev if her offer was still on the table. She said of course.

"So, despite being afraid of leaving the loving community I had gotten so familiar with, I went for it.

"I wasn't inclined to hide the nature of my relationship with Bev to Dave and Mary. But they didn't take it too well…They, unfortunately, were too brainwashed by the Church, like I'd been. I went and lived with Beverly, and became estranged from my brother's family in the process. I wasn't expecting that from them, after all the years we spent together. It broke my heart. But I still thanked them for taking me in when I needed it.

"Moving to Ottawa and living with Beverly was a massive change for me. I was fascinated with the city life. Not always a positive fascination, sometimes it was more like a curiosity with something that was strange and alien. I eventually got a job as a cleaner, at the hospital where Beverly worked.

"What stood out the most from those early days, was how excited I was for this new dimension in our relationship… That part felt like a dream. We'd spend a lot of our time at the library. My friends said that my vocabulary had become all high-falutin' with all the readin' and crosswords I'd been doing. Ha! We also spent our days cooking, exploring the city, visiting our hometowns here and there, hosting dinners with new friends. We could grow together.

"Not to say that we didn't have our challenges. It was real difficult, at times, to be in a relationship with someone who had all this unhealed trauma, y'know. It helped me to separate Bev's pain from Bev as a person. If you're safe—you just have to love 'em unconditionally, whether or not they're ready to heal.

At this point, Yoyo looked into the distance, tears quietly flowing down her face again. "I feel so blessed that I got spend two decades together with the love of my life—before she passed away from cancer," she said. "Sometimes I wish I could have helped her more. I honestly believe her body was rebelling against all that internalized shame," Yoyo said, wiping her cheek.

"I was lucky to have my support network around, to help me through my grieving. Dave and Mary also heard about what happened, and came back into my life. They apologized for disappearing in the first place.

"Still, it was a difficul' period. I felt like I was going through the motions for a very long time. After a couple of years, I felt like the clouds parted enough that I could snap out of autopilot, and assess what I was really doing.

"Bev had left me modest sum of money that I hadn't touched yet. I had been nursing a dream for a while, to open a bookstore. I considered the possibility of actually doin' it. That money gave me the confidence to go for it.

"I didn't have anything to lose, really. I could either continue in my unsatisfying ways, or go for the dream. I wanted to create a space where people could feel at home, understand themselves, grow. I felt like there wasn't enough places like that in the city. After envisioning it for so long, when I finally went for it—watchin' it come to life was… surreal.

Yoyo calmly took a sip of her tea. "And here we are," she said. "That answer your question?"

Shelia blinked, surprised to find herself at the end of Yoyo's backstory. She sat back up, having been leaning in the whole time. She felt heavy.

"Yoyo, you've been through so much. You are so fucking strong," Shelia said. "How can you even listen to me with all of my stupid, insignificant problems?"

"Pain and trauma are relative, Shelia. If you're not used to a hard life, something that seems minor in comparison will still shake ya. While Natives get the lion's share of the violence of this country, no one can live in this society and be unscathed. It'll just be a lot more subtle, eh. Like worshippin' money at the expense of yer wellbein'. Like isolation. Like tryin' to find meaning in meanin'less things. That's why I'm doing what I'm doing, to help people navigate the hurts of this world."

Shelia let Yoyo's words sink in. She looked at the old bookkeeper, and felt a new appreciation for her. "Thank you for doing that, Yoyo," Shelia said quietly. "Thank you for sharing your story with me."

"Yer welcome," Yoyo got up, clapping Shelia on the back. Shelia remained seated, sipping her tea. "Hey Yoyo," she called out after a while, "you remember that crappy book I bought from you?"

Yoyo raised an eyebrow for her to continue. Shelia pulled out the letter from her purse. "I found this inside it. Kind of random," she said offhandedly.

Yoyo came over and took a look at the letter. "Huh," she said. "You should give it to this lady's mom. Bet it'd make her day." She chuckled, "When you do, do let me know how loony Miss Moony is."

It was Thursday afternoon. She'd spent the day browsing on the internet. Now, she mulled over Olivia's invite. *Today. At seven. A How to Spring Back from Getting Your Ass Fired session hosted by Olivia.* Shelia's first instinct would be to not go, but then she considered what else she'd be doing. *More internet? Sending my résumé for the millionth time? Watching another inane reality show?* She could, of course, be hanging out at Yoyo's… if she didn't take Yoyo's subtle suggestions to get a life to heart. Thus, she grudgingly decided to go.

: I'm coming. See you soon.

A few seconds later, Olivia replied back.

Olivia: Great! See you.

A few minutes after seven, Shelia parallel parked by 42nd and Faraway, noting the cobblestone streets beneath her. She hadn't been to this part of town before, and she had to admit, it was nice. It was older, and a bit more cramped: but this made it cozier.

Shelia wore a cotton plum dress, and slightly upped her make up game. She wanted to seem the opposite of unemployed, and suggest that she may, in fact, be better than ever before.

Never the fuck mind if she was actually doing better.

"Hiii, Shelia," Olivia said warmly. "So glad you made it. Everyone else is here too." Olivia led her down a hallway, into her living room. Shelia noted hardwood floors and a Persian-inspired rug lining the hallway. Her old coworkers, plus some other people that she did not know, were all seated on couches that surrounded a food-laden table.

"Heyy," Jeremiah greeted. Elizabeth waved, and Lily ran up and gave Shelia a hug.

"Oh my god, how have you been?" Lily exclaimed. Shelia blinked. "Um... Decent," she nodded. "You?"

"Pfft. Broke, jobless. Not a good situation," she said lightly. "At least there's the severance package."

Olivia put her hand on Lily's shoulder. "Well, that's why we're here." She turned to Shelia, and gestured to the couch. "Go on, sit down. We have chips and dip. And alcohol," she added slyly.

Shelia sat herself down next to an unknown woman, fixing her dress as she did so. She nodded and smiled her signature non-smile at her, who smiled back. Shelia felt remarkably awkward. *What the hell am I doing here?* She noted that Mark was not present. Presumably because he was still employed.

"Hey everyone. So glad you all made it," she beamed, sitting herself next to Shelia. "So, I bet you're wondering what it is we're doing here…"

"Drinking disguised as networking," Jeremiah posited, putting his arm around Elizabeth.

Olivia laughed. "Well. I was thinking of this as more of a support group for people in economically troubled times. Air grievances, triumphs, and whatnot…" she said. "Who wants to go first?"

"Okay, well," Jeremiah started gamely, "As some of you know, I've been laid off. I've had to pick up my old bartending gig," he shrugged. "The bright side to this is that I've had more time to work on the program that Elizabeth and I were tinkering with at our job."

A balding dude sitting next to Lily asked, "What kind of program is it?"

"It's basically an add-on program that helps other programs run more efficiently," Elizabeth said.

"Hmm, tell me more about it."

Wow. Already some connections happening, Shelia mused.

"And how's the job front with you, Shelia? The rabble-rouser who quit before they had a chance to unceremoniously dump you?" Olivia grinned.

Shelia couldn't help but smile at the grand description that Olivia had bestowed on her. "Um," Shelia said. "Well. I've

110

applied to like, forty jobs. I've had some responses, but they seem to lead nowhere. So… yeah," she concluded, taking a chip. People nodded sympathetically.

"So what have you been up to in the meantime?" Lily asked.

Shelia poured herself a glass. "Uh… well…besides applying for jobs…" she paused, "I've been hanging out at a bookstore a lot."

She could tell people wanted a bit more of an explanation, but she left it at that. She did want to go into Yoyo's incredible backstory, but she felt awkward trying to articulate what her situation was with Yoyo's books.

Eventually the group conversation turned towards other topics. The woman sitting next to her pulled out of the group discussion and said to Shelia, "Tell me more about this bookstore."

"Well," Shelia said. "It's not just any bookstore. It's a bookstore run by this woman named Yoyo. She's like a tough-talking Yoda. And she takes people under her wing, I guess. There's like this whole hub of people she's created around the place. And her backstory, Jesus. She went from fleeing residential school and abusive relationships to running a bookstore. It's incredible."

"Wow," the woman said. "That does sound incredible. I'm surprised that more people don't know about the bookstore, given its backstory," she said thoughtfully. She took a sip of wine. "And—forgive me, what was your name again?"

"It's Shelia," she smiled. "You?"

"Amber," she replied. Amber asked Shelia for a business card. Shelia didn't have one, so she gave Amber her number in lieu of that. Shelia couldn't remember the last time she gave her number out, to new friends or potential lovers alike. Amber gave Shelia her business card, which read 'Amber Burns - Journalist'.

"Thanks for inviting me," Shelia said to Olivia, on her way out. "I had a good time." She meant it.

"Of course," Olivia said warmly.

5

Joel, one of the 2 am guys who was currently at Yoyo's during its daytime hours, slid his rook five spaces to the right. "Checkmate," he said.

"What?" Shelia said, mouth agape. "Ohhh, snap, Joel. You're right. Damn," she said.

"You put up a good fight though," Joel offered.

"Yeah, well, I used to be in the chess club in high school..." Shelia said. "You're so good though. I'm impressed."

"Lots of prac—" he was interrupted by the sound of the door suddenly flying open.

"Justin, it doesn't matter what they say," Monica said, as she and Justin barged in. "Just ignore them!"

"That's easy for you to say, you don't have to deal with it!"

He power-walked away from Monica and forcefully slumped into a seat at the back.

"Justin!" Monica said. She looked at Yoyo, expressing exasperation towards her friend.

I wonder what's going on? Shelia thought, as she put the chess pieces away.

Yoyo caught Shelia's and Monica's eyes, as if to say, *'Don't worry—I got this.'*

Yoyo got up, grabbed some tea, and sat across from Justin. She didn't say anything immediately, allowing them both to sit in silence for a while.

"So, Justin," Yoyo finally said. "What's the matter?"

Justin sighed. "They're... they're calling me gay. They're calling me a fag," he said, voice cracking.

"Oh, hun," she said, shaking her head. "Those bastards."

"They think me and my friend Sam are into each other, but we're not, we're just friends!" he said emphatically.

"Mhm," Yoyo nodded, stirring her tea. "When people say hurtful things to us, the worst part about it is when it crawls inside you and you believe it for yourself. That something about how you are, or how they think you are, is wrong. The fact that they're using bein' gay as an insult... just shows how brainwashed and ignorant they are," Yoyo said. "You know, being two-spirit always held a sacred space in our societies before colonialism came in and labelled it 'immoral'. I'm two-spirit myself. I do a lot of work restoring the traditional, spiritual role that we've always had."

"Really?" Justin said, eyes wide. "I didn't know that, Yoyo."

"You betcha," she said proudly. "And believe me, I've faced a lot of heck for it," she cackled. "Listen, Justin. I believe in you to stand up to them however you see fit, but the best defence will be to realize, and internalize, the truth. When someone says something negative towards you, the reason it hurts is because that negativity couldn't be further from the true nature of who you are—but part of you, maybe a very small part, wonders if the negativity is true. When you know the truth, nothing anyone can say can touch ya. Do you understand?"

Justin nodded. "Yeah... but it's hard, though."

"I know, sweetie," Yoyo said. "But I believe in you. And listen, don't hesitate to come on back here if you get any more problems with this."

"I know, Yoyo," he smiled.

Yoyo clapped him on the back and left him to do his own thing.

Shelia, digesting that interaction, pondered Yoyo's words. *The reason it hurts is because that negativity couldn't be further from the true nature of who you are.*

"Yoyo strikes again," Shelia said appreciatively to Yoyo, as she passed by. "How do you do it?"

"Lots of practice."

Shelia glanced at her GPS. *Alright, Rivercrest is on...* she thought, changing her lane, *my right...* She turned into the retirement home at the appropriate exit. The whole area was unfamiliar to her: Shelia hardly ever went to the south side. Walking in, Shelia was struck by the horrible pastel palette of the place.

"Excuse me," Shelia said to the receptionist, letter in hand. "Is… um…" she suddenly realized how ridiculous it was to ask for someone whose actual name you didn't know. But she didn't have any other choice. "…a Miss Moon here?" she finally asked. Shelia braced herself for a look of confusion and weirded-outness from the receptionist.

Instead, the receptionist said, "Room 408. You can sign the visitor's book over there," she said, cocking her head to the left.

Shelia thought about asking the receptionist about why Miss Moon was called Miss Moon, but she vetoed the motion in her head. She signed the book and headed for room 408, traversing mint-coloured hallways on her way.

Shelia hesitated before the door, the '408' featured in bold, black numerals. *Right. What's the point of doing this? There… is no point but to make an old lady's day better?*

She knocked, but there was no answer. After pausing for a moment, she decided to go in.

Shelia was met with the sight of a frail older woman, lying in bed, peering at Shelia. Shelia blinked back at Miss Moon.

"Hi…" Shelia started. She remembered the letter she was clutching, and held it up. "So… I found this letter, from your daughter, in a used book I bought," Shelia said.

Shelia waited for Miss Moon's response, but all she did was look at Shelia blankly.

"Um..." Shelia said awkwardly. "Right. So, here you go," she said, gently handing Miss Moon the letter.

Miss Moon took it slowly—suspiciously—scrutinizing the letter. Her etched eyes widened. "How...do you have this? Who...are you?" she asked, breathing in between words.

Dude, I just said—Oh. It occurred to Shelia that Miss Moon might not have been hearing anything she was saying.

"I'M SHELIA," she shouted. "I BROUGHT A LETTER FROM YOUR DAUGHTER—I FOUND IT IN A BOOK."

Instead of showing signs of recognizing what Shelia had just said, Miss Moon's face was back to blank.

Shelia sighed. She scanned the room, and zoomed in on a stray unused napkin. Pulling out a pen from her bag, she scrawled on the napkin what she had just futilely yelled out. She then handed the napkin with its encoded message to Miss Moon.

After Miss Moon read the napkin, she turned her head and grinned at Shelia, to Shelia's surprise. "Oh...how wonderful...And it was...found in a book, you say?" she said, delighted. Miss Moon reached for the letter resting on her lap and said, "My eyesight isn't...too sharp...these days, and my daughter did...always write so darn tiny. Would you mind reading it out loud for me, dear?"

Shelia nodded with a polite smile. When Shelia finished her narration with a "Love, Candace," Miss Moon was smiling. "Thank you, dear," she said. It was a sad smile.

Shelia shut the door behind her and walked back to her car, feeling unsettled. Once seated in the car, she noticed that her phone was blinking.

Mei: I'm going to come visit you next weekend! There's an Octopi and Wallace show in Ottawa that I want to check out.

Shelia's first thought was *shit*. She immediately realized that she'd forgotten to tell her family that she was unemployed. She rubbed her forehead. *Ugh, I am not looking forward to her reaction.* She reversed her car out of its parking spot and headed home.

For the first time since ever, Shelia found herself at Yoyo's before Yoyo herself. She'd woken up with a caged-in feeling that made her have to leave her apartment. *Normal people would go to coffee shops in this situation, but I go to closed bookstores...*

Which is why she was currently on her knees, carefully applying white paint to the front door with the three-by-three paneling. Each stroke she made was strangely soothing. Shelia jumped when Yoyo said behind her, "What happened to creatin' that database doohickey?"

"Uh...what?" Shelia said, snapping out of her painting reverie. She looked at Yoyo, confused. "Yoyo? Why are you outside right now?" Shelia knew that Yoyo always slept in, in response to her night owl hours.

"I went to get the mail," Yoyo replied, not asking Shelia what she herself was doing here at this hour. "I couldn't sleep, anyway," she mumbled. Yoyo made a move towards the door and Shelia got out of the way, paint bucket in hand. *Something is off,* Shelia thought, mulling over this difference in energy she felt from Yoyo. But she couldn't place it.

"It's not bad," Yoyo said, once they were both inside. "The paint job."

"Not bad" meant solid approval, and normally Shelia would be pleased at such a rare thing as Yoyo's approval. But Yoyo said it with a massive frown.

"Uh... thanks..." Shelia said, scrutinizing Yoyo for clues into her psyche. Yoyo hobbled over to her desk and slumped into her chair, heaving a massive sigh.

"Yoyo... is everything alright?" She asked tentatively. The words felt strange coming out of her mouth, because she wasn't sure if she'd ever uttered them before.

Yoyo looked at Sheila, her eyebrows furrowed. "They're forcing renovations and the rent is being raised, and I can't afford to stay here anymore. Truth be told... I've been treading water for a long time now," she sighed. "Supporters have been generous enough to keep this thing alive, but it's not a way to sustain a business. This time, it's over."

Shelia didn't really believe what Yoyo was saying. It felt like it was something coming from a different dimension.

So she resisted it. "But they can't raise the rent like that."

"Yes, they can."

"If supporters have kept it alive all these years, they'd do it again," Sheila tried instead, crossing her arms.

Yoyo shook her head. "They ain't rich either. I can't ask them to keep doing this."

Shelia frowned, her mind turning to think of a rebuttal.

Yoyo just gave her a faint smile. "Don't you worry about me, missy. I'll be alright."

But what about us? Will we be alright?

"There's one more thing," Yoyo said, before Sheila could bug her again. "We'll be open for two more months. Of course, yer invited to the closing hoopla... But for one month after today, ya can't come in here and help out," Yoyo said simply.

Sheila blinked, computing what Yoyo just said. "Wait. So you're... banning me?" she asked, still confused.

"Because I think you're relying on this as yer anchor too much."

"That's why you're kicking me out?" Shelia said, incredulous. The losing of cool was immediate. "SO WHAT if I'm using this as an anchor?" she erupted. "What else do you want me to do? I'm unemployed, and I have no friends! I'll go insane unless I have some stupid anchor!"

Yoyo didn't mirror Shelia's anger in her response. "Comfort zones are not for you right now. You've spent yer whole life in one," she noted. Smiling, she said, "You're a tough cookie, Shelia—you'll figure it out."

Shelia scoffed, unimpressed. "Ugh, just stop it with all of this wise guru crap. I want you to be my friend, not my *sensei*."

"I'm saying this as yer friend, Shelia. And your sensei," she winked.

She did not mirror Yoyo's amicability back. "Well, guess what? Friends don't ban each other from their establishments. But hey, I might as well get a head start on getting out of that comfort zone, so you know what? I'll just leave right now. Yeah," she said, getting up.

"Let me know how it goes," Yoyo said affably. "At the closing party."

Shelia glared at Yoyo in response. She shut the door forcefully, rattling the small bell into a frenzy.

The outside air harshly met her face. Shelia started walking at random, not knowing where she was going. After a block, Shelia's anger dissipated, leaving her feeling like she'd behaved like a toddler having a tantrum. *Yeah, it's annoying to be kicked out. But Yoyo is technically old. It's a little uncouth to get mad at old people.* She sighed, halting her walking. *What am I going to do now?*

She went home and spent the rest of the evening watching Vengeful Mamas.

At this point in her life, Shelia may have fallen into a bonafide, anchorless rock-bottom, if it weren't for a text from Amber.

Hi Shelia, this is Amber from Olivia's "Recession Support Group". So, my professional website could use a makeover and I don't really want to hire a random from the internet. Could I hire you for the job?

Shelia felt the rare feeling of excitement. *A job!* She had sent about forty applications since quitting Cogville, with twenty responses (all of them leading nowhere, except one that required her to move to Minnesota), and it took just one Olivia Get-Together to land her a gig.

Well, my thing is coding software, but I could do websites too. I'm a woman of many talents.

Shelia and Amber set up a time to meet up and discuss the work to be done, and Shelia felt a the rare feeling of being satisfied. After that faded, however, she was faced with what she should do with the rest of her day. The rest of her week.

What the hell do people do with their time?

She presumed they (i.e, people who were not awkward fucks like herself) hung out with their S.O, their friends, maybe their kids.

She pinched her muffin top, as she occasionally did. Shelia always was relatively skinny despite not exercising, but she considered if that was what she should do with her time.

Mental health benefits and all. And I could get rid of my muffin top. She considered going for a run.

Man, runs are so boring though. Maybe a class? But she hadn't factored in gym fees into her unemployment fund. She opened up her finances out of curiosity.

Dear God. When she looked at her balance, the amount had indeed dwindled at a rate she'd technically expected... but it had all been theory before now. Actually being confronted with her shrinking funds made her stomach feel cold. *I really thought I would have found a job by now... Okay. So definitely no gym membership then,* she sighed.

She slumped into her couch. She started browsing the internet without thinking, scrolling through page after page on her phone.

Racially motivated hate crime kills couple in South Carolina.

Canadian dollar plunges further.

Study shows that socially isolated individuals die about 15% earlier than their connected counterparts.

Shelia continued scrolling, and then doubled-back to the isolation study. *Wow. Great.*

Shelia felt that the familiar adage "Time flies when you're having fun!" was false. In fact, she found the opposite to be true. *Time flies when your life sucks ass.* Her days had become amorphous blobs, all bleeding into each other, and when she looked at the time or date she was constantly surprised. She didn't like the feeling that time was zooming past her at breakneck speed.

Fortunately for Shelia, the blob days were broken up by her meeting with Amber, and she was grateful.
They met in the same hipstery neighbourhood where she'd met Dipon a month ago.

"So, I'm going for a black and white minimalistic look. Really classic."
Shelia nodded in between sips of coffee. "I see…" She pulled out a notepad and pen she had in her bag, and started drawing. Amber watched attentively.

"So this could be the header… toolbar…" Shelia said, in-between scribbling, "and when you click on one of links… it'll look like… this."
Amber nodded approvingly. "That looks great. When do you think you could have it done by?"
Pfft. This is child's play. "Within two days," Shelia said amicably.

"That's great. And how much will it be?"
Shelia blanked for a second. She hadn't really thought about the price. "I'd say…that five hundred dollars makes sense for a project of this scope," she said, trying to sound professional.
Amber smiled. "Great," she said, getting up. "Thanks for meeting up with me, Shelia."

"Yeah, of course," Shelia smiled back. Shelia waved to Amber on her way out. Shelia stayed put and immediately went to work, feeling better than she had since she'd been kicked out of Yoyo's. A couple of hours later and she was done. Shelia held off on contacting Amber immediately, lest she think that Shelia was overeager (which she was, of course.)

Man. Maybe I should have procrastinated more, Shelia thought as she steadily approached her apartment. She dreaded the return to the endless boring nothingness.

She got out of her car and dragged herself to the building entrance. Once she got there, she stood in front of the doors, immobile. *Fuck it. I'm not going back in there to continue the saga of wasting my days away.*

She started walking furiously away from the building, once again not knowing where she was going. She had a sense of déja vu as she did this. She tucked her hands into her pockets, watching her breath fog in front of her face.

A few minutes into her directionless walking, she had a sense of calm that had been absent in her of late. *Man, I should have gone for a walk a long time ago.* All that time she'd known such an activity would be good for her, but she'd resisted. Because it didn't seem worth it to overcome the inertia to leave the house when it was cold and one had Netflix.

She eventually found herself nearing Yoyo's and took care to avoid it. This led her to landing in a nearby residential area, where the houses were small and stuccoed.

A brown dog ran up to the front fence of one of the houses and barked inquisitively at her, looking as if it were waiting for something. Shelia slowly went up to the dog and hesitantly patted its head, and continued on her way.

A white couple with a stroller passed her by. Shelia was caught off-guard when they smiled at her, and by the time she smiled back it was too late for them to notice.

Soon she wound up passing by a school—middle or junior?—and she was alarmed by the sheer volume of young humans running around. *Is it recess?* she pondered. *No… it's late afternoon—guess school's out for the day.*

"Holy shit, it's Shelia!" a voice hollered.

Shelia spun around to locate the source of the voice. Until she did, her mind was a swirl of questions: *Who knew her here? And what, exactly, was so special about me that prompted a "holy shit"?*

"Oh my god, Justin, Monica," Shelia said, once her eyes spotted their familiar faces. Shelia hadn't recognized the voice as Justin's immediately.

"What are you doing here?!" Monica exclaimed, giving her a hug (which Shelia was not expecting).

"Uh… I'm just going for a walk. And I guess… you guys go to school here?"

"Yeah. Unfortunately. Can't wait til I can blow this shithole," Monica grumbled. *She better be staying in this shithole until she graduates,* Shelia thought.

"I haven't seen you at the shop in a while," Justin noted.

"Ah, well…" Shelia started. "That's because I've been kicked out by Yoyo. Because I apparently go there too much,"

Shelia said dryly. As soon as she said it, she'd felt as if she'd violated some woman-code: bad-mouthing Yoyo to the kids (even if it was just through her sassy tone) felt improper.

"Huh," Monica said. "She's kicking you out right before Yoyo's closes down?"

"Well, she is letting me go to the closing party." Monica and Justin nodded.

"Oh guess what Shelia, Justin told those bullies that they were colonial motherfuckers and they backed off," Monica informed her.

"Wow, that's awesome," Shelia grinned.

"I mean, they still bother me sometimes, but I'm better at not letting it affect me," he shrugged. "Anyways," he said enterprisingly, "I'm glad I ran into you, Shelia. 'Cause I got an idea that will save Yoyo's." Monica groaned, knowing of the idea already (and disapproving of it).

"No, listen, it could totally work," he reassured Monica. To Shelia, he said, "How about... you teach us how to make a video game, and then we sell it and use the money for Yoyo's?"

Upon hearing Justin's grand plan, Shelia discreetly locked eyes with Monica's, which said, *"See, I told you he was a ridiculous fuck."*

Shelia agreed that Justin's grand plan might be a bit unrealistic, but she certainly didn't want to let him know that. *He's so full of youthful hope and optimism....*

"Well, I mean… while I can't really control market demand, which is notoriously fickle, I can definitely teach you guys how to make a video game," is what Shelia ended up saying.

"Awesome," Justin said.

Shelia wouldn't have guessed that Justin would be the type to be into designing video games, and she felt his enthusiasm rubbing off on her. Monica, on the other hand, still looked skeptical.

"Yeah, I mean, I guess you guys can come over Monday after your classes. Here's my address and phone number," Shelia said, writing it down on a stray, unused napkin she had in her pocket.

"Hey, we'll get to see where the mysterious Shelia lives!" Monica said excitedly.

Mysterious? "Pfft. Me? The mystery is that I watch Vengeful Mamas all day."

"Ohmigosh me too!" Monica said. "Did you catch that episode where Kaitlin threw up in front of her ex's new wife's family?"

"Um, yes. That was mortifying!" Shelia found herself inexplicably excited that she had found a kindred soul to dish about Vengeful Mamas with.

"I don't know! She owned it. And then she ended up grinding on that hot dude."

"Uh…" Shelia said, remembering something. "Wasn't that guy only a couple of years older than her son?"

"Oh… um, yeah, I guess. But he was still pretty cute."

Man, reality TV is such a bad influence. "Um… Right. Well. I'll see you guys Monday then. Have a good weekend," she said, walking away.

"See you, Mrs. Teacher," Justin called out.

"Still Shelia."

"Yeah, Justin. Shelia's not one of those regular teachers— she's a cool teacher," Monica said.

Shelia rolled her eyes, smiling.

She continued wandering around. Here and there she would stop into random establishments to warm up, staying as long as acceptably possible without buying anything. Sometimes the sales people made small talk with her, and she obliged them. She was grateful for the human contact, even if it was all small talk. Shelia found it notable that when she stopped in a 7-Eleven, a lady offered her a pizza slice. Shelia would normally be suspicious, but she was too numbed out from the cold to overthink things.

"Um… Wow. Thanks."

Nibbling on her pizza, she came across a fire hydrant that was shaped like an asparagus stalk and wondered what the meaning of it was. This was the about the point where she realized it was eight and she'd wandered extremely far away from her apartment, and the mere idea of walking all the way back exhausted her. She begrudgingly started to call a cab, not looking forward to the bill at the end, when a bus blared past her. *Right. Buses are a thing…*

Once aboard, Shelia found herself enraptured in the makeup of her fellow passengers. *Wow. Ottawans are actually really good looking,* she thought. It made her vaguely insecure about her own looks.

She was also surprised by how much French she heard. *I mean, that makes sense, we're right next to Quebec... how come I've never noticed before?... I guess I've just been in an anglophone bubble.*

Upon reaching her apartment, Shelia slumped to bed immediately, exhausted by the one-and-a-half-hour commute. With a jolt she realized she hadn't sent Amber her updated website and dragged herself out of bed to do so. Within minutes Amber responded,

Shelia, this amazing. I don't need any modifications, it's awesome as it is.

Sending you the commission via e-transfer. Thanks so much!

Shelia was pleased. She no longer felt sleepy, so she passed the time by watching Vengeful Mamas until the fatigue washed over her once again.

The day that Octopi and Wallace came to Ottawa was firmly upon Shelia, and with it, a visit from her sister.

"Hiiiiii, Shelia," Mei greeted, hugging her. Shelia inspected her younger sibling: she looked the same as usual. Mei plopped her bag and jacket onto the couch: an action that made Shelia cringe a little.

"Mei, I have a coat rack, you know," Shelia said, pointing at said coat rack (pointedly).

Mei rolled her eyes, picked up her jacket and (pointedly) plopped it on the coat rack.

"You know, whenever I come here, your place is like… robotically clean. It kind of creeps me out. You don't have to clean so much for when I visit," Mei said.

"Uh… I didn't clean for you?" Shelia said immediately.

"That makes it even creepier."

"Alright then," Shelia snapped, "Next time I'll make sure my place is a pigsty, just for you, sis."

Mei sighed in response and seated herself on the couch. A tense silence permeated the apartment. After a while, Shelia broke it by asking Mei if she wanted some food.

"Yeah, actually, that would be great. Thanks."

"Okay…" Shelia said, opening her fridge. "I have some pasta, leftover pizza, and some salad?"

"Pasta and salad sound great."

Shelia brought a plate for herself and Mei, taking a seat across from her. She switched on the television and put on another episode of the dramedy she'd already had going.

"Carmella, maybe you should just stop fucking guys twice your age."

"Have you considered that maybe I'm just working through my daddy issues, Jamie? Or even, like, general life issues?"

After the show was over, Mei asked, "Got any plans for tonight?"

"Nope," she replied.

"Really, no hot date?" Mei pressed.

"Hmm, must have missed the decree that One Must Go Out on Fridays."

Mei rolled her eyes, but was undeterred from her line of questioning. "Shelia, like... who is your crew? I don't know anything about what you do in your spare time, for fun."

"I don't know, I just quit my job. I'm readjusting my life, I guess."

Mei looked at her, incredulous. "*What?* You quit your job?! How come you didn't mention it before? What are you doing for money??"

"Freelancing," Shelia said nonchalantly.

She definitely felt the weird role-reversal that was going on: usually, Shelia was the neurotic one and Mei, the carefree one. *Who am I kidding? I'm still freaked out as fuck. But there's no way I'm gonna let that on to Mei.*

Mei still looked concerned. "Did you tell Ma and Ba yet?"

Mei's line of questioning went from mildly annoying Shelia to pissing her off. "Listen, I don't need you to act all concerned for me. It's pretty condescending."

"I guess you didn't tell them then."

"It doesn't matter if I told them or not. *You* can't just come and stay in *my* apartment and then act so patronizing."

131

"I am not being patronizing," Mei said. "I'm asking because I care. I just asked normal questions—you're overreacting."

"Care in a way that's less irritating," Shelia snapped. "Or go and "care" somewhere else."

"What the hell is wrong with you?" Mei shot. "Only *you* would have a problem with caring," she said, slamming the bathroom door and shutting herself in.

When she came out, she was all made up. She collected her purse and jacket and said, "I'm going to go the show now. Have fun by yourself."
Shelia felt her face go hot at *"by yourself"*, but tried to portray aloofness. "Insults me, expects to stay over…"

"Oh, so do I have to go and book a hotel room, now?"
Shelia glared at Mei and didn't say anything. Mei turned around and slammed the door behind her.
Shelia turned around and promptly laid on the floor. She felt drained. *Family is overrated,* she thought bitterly. *All it means is that people are entitled to be assholes and you still have to hang out with them anyway.*
Mei's prodding forced open the anxieties and insecurities Shelia had been burying.
I've been unemployed for two months… and all I've managed to do is work one small gig. And I wouldn't have even gotten that gig if it weren't for Olivia… And it's not like I've been using that time to fix my social life. I still have no friends, no lovers… Fuck, what the fuck is wrong with me?! What was I doing this whole time? Hanging out

132

at a fucking bookstore with a cryptic old lady who would end up
dumping me anyway? I haven't just wasted these two months. I've
wasted my whole life.

Tears spilled out of her eyelids and onto her ears. A thought
loop of *you're pathetic, you've wasted your life,* played in her
head until another voice said amidst the noise, sharply, *Stop*
being an asshole to yourself. The loop stopped in its tracks.

I can't, Shelia thought in response.

Just try.

No. I can't. My life sucks and its my own stupid fault. The loop
continued.

Enough already! the other voice said. *Just take a breath.*

Shelia, inexplicably, did as she was told. *Inhale, exhale. Inhale,*
exhale. The loop subsided. Shelia sighed. She shifted onto her
hip. This move brought her face to face with *A Practical Guide*
to Life, which was lying on the floor as well. *Well, what do you*
know, Maria Walker, Shelia thought dryly. *I stopped being an*
asshole to myself. Briefly.

Shelia decided to peruse the table of contents. The chapter
entitled "Friends" caught Shelia's eye.

FRIENDS: HOW THE FUCK TO DEAL WITH THEM (OR THE LACK THEREOF)

'Loneliness is the fucking human condition. Accept that. But the #1 rule is you have to be comfortable in your own company. (See 'Stop Being an Asshole to Yourself' for tips on how to build your relationship with yourself.)

However, humans are social creatures. The other #1 rule is quality over quantity, always. Always make nurturing the relationships that make your heart sing a priority.

The caveat is that you should keep your social life dynamic. If you like it how it is, great, but remember that comfort = death (this is true for everything, basically). Make sure you have a chance to meet new people. Definitely go to parties — even if you don't feel like going all the time. Sometimes you just need to force yourself to go for your own good. Go especially if they're thrown by a friend. They will probably know people that you will like.

Friends come from unexpected places. Be open to people who are out of your "zone" — be it politics, age, or socioeconomic background. These friendships are gold because each of the people in them can learn a lot from each other.

"Eh" friends and what to do with them: I wouldn't say to dump them like toxic friends (which we will cover shortly). Mainly because there's a chance that with time the friendship will

deepen as you guys slowly learn about each other. And if not—
they might invite you to parties.

When you actually have 0 friends: The #1 rule in this situation is
to not be hard on yourself. It does not fucking help, and it is rude
to yourself, so don't do it. In a gentle manner you can analyze
why this situation came to be. The most common reason is that
you've moved to a new place. People who are hard on
themselves who've moved to a new city are dumb because, what
do you expect? It takes a lot of fucking time to build a good
social network. Be patient, for Christ's sake. The best thing to do
is go to events. There are many groups online that organize
events based on interest. Remember that friend-making is
cumulative, though. You may go to an event, and connect
superficially with people. It would be a mistake to deem this a
failure. The more people you meet, the more likely you'll run
into someone again. And it might be by the second or third or
fourth encounter, that you'll form a genuine connection.

And if you've been living in the same place for ten years and still
feel like you have 0 friends: be patient, have an open heart. The
case for you folks is probably that you have more friends than
you think. They've just fallen by the wayside or haven't been
given a chance to develop. This is what you do:

Write down a list of all the people, if you saw them randomly,
you would say hi to. Preferably because you want to, not out of
obligation.

Send those people an email, text, facebook message, whatever, saying "Hey! It's been a while. How are you doing?" or something like that.

Then, once a rapport is established, invite them for coffee. (Note that people are fickle and that it is possible you'll only reach rapport with 1 out of every 10 people you reach out to.)'

Shelia sighed. *Alright, 'Practical Guide to Life'.* She pulled out her phone.

Hey! It's been a while. How's it going?, Shelia typed. She was immediately disgusted by its implied enthusiasm and backspaced the message into oblivion.

Hey., she typed instead. Hows the program coming along. Shelia pressed send, feeling accomplished socially. *Will Jeremiah get back to me? According to Walker, only 1 out of 10 people do.* Shelia wondered who else she should message. She scrolled through her contact list in search of potential friends. *Okay, there's Lily, maybe... Oh, and Mark...* When Olivia's number showed up, Shelia quickly scrolled away. A few seconds later, she scrolled back to it, but she couldn't bring herself to message her. She reached the end of her contact list, dismayed by how pitiful the amount of Ottawans she knew was.

After deliberating on it for a bit, she texted Lily a Hey. It's been a while. How are you? She sent Mark a similar message. She regarded the screen for a second before tucking her phone into her pocket.

'If all else fails and you still feel crushing loneliness—it's okay. Feel it, accept it, wallow in it for a bit. Then stop and think of one person you can help right now. As Eve Ensler says, "you must give what you want most in the world in order to heal the broken parts inside of yourself." Giving will help you get outside of your goddamn head (in a constructive way). It will help you realize the wealth that is inside of you, always.'

She fell asleep reading more of 'A Practical Guide to Life'. She dreamt that she was strangling Yoyo's death-and-taxes rubber chicken.

The dream abruptly gave way to the sound of ringing. "What?" she shot up, disoriented. "Oh…" she blinked, locating where her phone was. *It's Mei.* Her phone's white glow cooly displayed the time: past one-thirty.

"Yes?" she mumbled into the phone.

"Sorry for waking you, Shi-shi. Is it cool for me to stay over?… It was kind of left unclear."

"Um," she rubbed her eyes. "Yeah. Of course."

"Okay, cool," Mei said. "By the way, Shelia, I'm sorry." She added hastily, "And I'm not just saying that just so I can stay over or anything."

"Alright," Shelia said. "See you in a bit."

Shelia opened the door for Mei, when she returned a little while later. Shelia gave her an amicable nod and went straight back to sleep.

She slept in longer than she expected to. *I officially killed Yoyo's death-and-taxes chicken,* she thought hazily.

Mei was already in the kitchen, cooking. She was donning a newly acquired *Octopi and Wallace* T-shirt.

"I'm pretty sure the guest is not supposed to be the one cooking," Shelia noted, seating herself by the island.

"I'm pretty sure formalities are void when it comes to your siblings," Mei said. "Besides, I'm happy to do it. I felt bad for waking you up."

Shelia waved off Mei's guilt. *Am I still annoyed at Mei?* she thought. *Well, for one, she apologized. And I guess what she said bothered me mainly because I was already bothered by it myself.*

After they finished breakfast, Mei packed up her things.

"Thanks for hosting me, Shi-shi. I got you a little something," she said, slyly handing over a gift bag.

"Hmm, I thought formalities were void with siblings?"

When she pulled out what was inside, her jaw dropped. "Oh my god, Mei! *Why?*"

Shelia held up the 'Triple X G-Spot Toy by Seductionz' in consternation, before tucking it away in the gift bag again.

Mei shrugged. "Well, I mean, I don't know if you're getting any."

In response to this, Shelia felt the back of her neck go hot. Her little sister's judgement of her (lack of) sex life was too much for her. She felt embarrassed, and then she felt angry.

"This is exactly what I mean by your patronizing attitude," she said. "I swear, all of you think I'm just biding my time until I snag some man. Do you think I'm some poor, tragic figure, drowning in sexlessness?" She curtly gave the gift back to Mei. "I do not need your pity."

Shelia expected Mei to mirror her anger, but she softened, instead.

"I don't think you're a tragic figure, Sheel," she said. "I mean, I can see why you would think I saw you that way. But really, I just wasn't sure if you saw yourself as one."

Shelia had been ready to fire back, but this response? She was unprepared for. She blinked, unsure of what to say.

Exhaling, she said, "What makes you think I don't already have one of these, anyway?"

Mei laughed. "You can never have too many of 'em. Keep it," she insisted.

They tightly hugged each other goodbye. "Don't forget, it's your turn to visit now!" Mei called out, as she walked away.

"Giving will help you get outside your goddamn head in a constructive way," she thought, once again finding herself in the eerily mint-colored Rivercrest Retirement Home.

"Hey Miss Moon," she greeted.

Shelia readied herself for Miss Moon not knowing who she was, but instead Miss Moon replied, "You're that...Oriental girl from before who...brought me my daughter's letter."

Eh. I'll let that slide because she's old. "Name's Shelia," she said. She noted that Miss Moon was donning some hearing aids this time around. *Cool, don't have to shout everything.*

"Got more letters for me?" Miss Moon said.

"Uh. Well." *Jesus. This was a harebrained idea.* "Actually... I was wondering if you wanted someone to help you write letters to your kids."

"Oh..." Miss Moon blinked. "You know dear...if I wanted to do that...I could...ask the staff for help," Miss Moon pointed out.

Shelia, in fact, had not thought of this possibility. Miss Moon bringing it up made Shelia feel even more foolish for coming. "So... you don't want to write to your kids?"

Miss Moon looked uncomfortable. "It's...not that...I don't want to, it's simply unnecessary."

"Is... that because you communicate mostly through phone calls and real life visits and such, then?" Shelia asked, trying to figure out what Miss Moon meant.

The look on Miss Moon's face indicated that this was not the case. "It's...just unnecessary," she repeated.

Social protocol called for backing off on what was obviously a touchy subject, but Shelia couldn't get herself to.

"So... you and your kids sort of have a rocky relationship, huh?" Shelia said quietly.

Miss Moon didn't say anything.

Shelia didn't account for estrangement when she planned to help someone. She wasn't sure what to do next.

She cleared her throat. "I'm... sorry about that."

Miss Moon looked at her, and sighed. "In some...ways...not keeping in touch...made things easier..." she shook her head. "It just hits you when you get to my age."

This vague sad admission from Miss Moon intrigued Shelia, but she decided not to prod her further. In the absence of questioning Miss Moon, Shelia was not sure what to do or say, so she played with her fingers nervously.

So, my plan failed. I guess I should probably leave. "Right," Shelia started, making motions towards the door. "Well—"

"Wait one second, Missy," Miss Moon interrupted. "Do you know how to play crib?"

"Uh... no." Shelia wasn't sure if she even vaguely knew what crib was.

Miss Moon gingerly patted the side table beside her. Shelia decided to go along with this development, and pulled up a chair.

Four rounds later, Shelia asked, "So... why are you called Miss Moon?"

Miss Moon looked at her. "What?"

"Um... like, why is your name Miss Moon?"

Miss Moon looked at her confusedly. "Because my maiden name was Moon...and the staff here...took a liking to calling me 'Miss Moon'."

"Moon's, like… a real name? Huh." She took a card.

"Indeed it is," Moon responded, taking a card herself.

6

"Whoaaaaaa," Monica said, walking slowly around Shelia's apartment. "Nice place, dude."
Justin belly flopped onto Shelia's suede couch. Monica followed suit, plopping herself with similar enthusiasm.

"Ah… please be careful with the couch…!" Shelia thought of her pad as a pretty normal, standard place for a single gal. But through the eyes of fourteen-year olds, she could see how it could be magical.

"Right," Shelia said to them, hands on her hips, in what she hoped was a teacher-like pose. The two straightened up and regarded her like attentive pupils would, which Shelia found weirdly gratifying. Relaxing her posture, she sat on the arm of a nearby couch. As she did so, her phone emitted a tinny beep, indicating a text. *I'll check it later.*

"You know, I spent my undergrad learning mostly theory, which was fine, you know—but I learned so much more when I started working and actually started doing stuff. So what we're gonna do," Shelia said, pulling out her laptop, "is learn some basic concepts and then start applying them." She propped her laptop open, screen facing the kids, text editor open.

"The thing to keep in mind is that computers are like super pedantic toddlers. Unless you're extremely specific in what you want them to do, they'll fu—er, they'll mess things up."

"Oh my god Shelia, you know you can say 'fuck' around us," Monica interjected.

"Yeah. Fuck fuck fuck. See?" Justin added.

"Um, no, I don't want to be responsible for corrupting you guys further. Anyway," Shelia indicated to the monitor as Monica stuck out her tongue, "Let's start with 'Hello World'…"

As Monica and Justin took turns tinkering with the code, Shelia checked her phone.

Oh hey Shelia. Surprised to hear from you. Program is actually going quite well
We got some interested prospects
How are things with you?

Hey, Jeremiah replied… And it seems he and Elizabeth are getting traction with their program, cool.

"How are things with you?" Ugh, I hate this question. Obviously can't say that things are shitty.

That's great
I'm still on the job hunt! Picked up some freelancing gigs here and there.

Is what she ended up replying. Shelia was already jaded about how the conversation would run. *Jeremiah will say something like "oh, nice" or "good luck!" and that would be the end of that. What's the point? All of this is so use—*

"Shelia!!" Monica called out, snapping Shelia out of her brooding.

"What?"

"I did everything you told me to do and it's still not working," Monica said, looking dismayed at the blinking error message.

Shelia glanced it over. "You forgot to close that tag here," Shelia pointed out.

"Ohhhhhhhhhhhhhhhh."

"You know, what I usually do is type both the opening and closing tag at the same time and write all the stuff in between afterwards."

"Oooh, good tip," Monica said.

Monica fixed the incomplete tag and pressed 'enter'. A black screen with the words 'Hello Muthafuckas' in white appeared. Apparently Shelia'd missed that in her proofreading.

"Oh, I bet you're real pleased with yourself," Shelia said dryly. Monica grinned at her cheekily. "Fine, alright, good job, Monica," Shelia allowed. She turned to Justin, erasing all of the code that was just written. "Okay, you're up, Justin.

This time we can get into adjusting the colour and the size and the font and such…"

"Cool. When do we get to making a video game though?"

"We'll get to that. Just start here," Shelia said with an assured smile.

After a bit of instruction from her, the background noise filled with clicks and taps again. Shelia felt pleased wearing the hat of the knowledgable mentor. *Like they're the karate kid and I'm the sensei… Now I know how Yoyo feels.*

With the thought of Yoyo, Shelia felt a pang of resentment and sadness. She looked at her phone again as a means of distraction.

Jeremiah: Oh hey Shelia. Surprised to hear from you. Interface is going well

Jeremiah: How are things with you?

: Still on the job hunt! Picked up some freelancing gigs here and there.

Shelia hated the idea of letting this exchange go to conversation death. Impulsively, she sent another message.

You wanna catch up over drinks sometime? You can invite Elizabeth too. (As she typed, she vaguely overheard "Hey, you can't say muthafuckas, that's my thing," and Justin arguing back.)

Shelia wasn't the type to initiate hangouts. She was a little buzzed from doing something out of her comfort zone, but she wondered if her text broke the etiquette of casual friendship. *Ah, well, I guess it's out there now.*

"Hey Shelia!" Justin called out. "What do you think?" he asked expectantly.

Shelia took in the giant text of 'I can say muthafuckas if I want' in purple. She shook her head in mock disapproval. "I thought you were classier than Monica, Justin," she sighed. "But... good job," she smirked.

Shelia waved the kids goodbye when they were done their lesson. She gingerly shut the door behind them and relaxed into her couch. She actually felt... *content?*

Contentment had become such a foreign feeling to her that she was suspicious of it. Nonetheless, she used the resurgent energy to complete tasks such as email and paying her bills. One subject line in particular got her excited. *'Invitation to Interview'! Finally!*

When she got to her bills, she conversely felt a pit in her stomach grow as she she watched her bank account dwindle with every payment. As she completed her payments, her text message tone went off.

Sounds great, she read, checking her phone. Me and some friends are meeting up tomorrow at Sweeney's if you want to join, around 7.

Ugh, that means I have to buy drinks. She exhaled a stress breath. *It's okay, I can afford it, I can afford it...*

Cool, sounds good. see you then. she replied.

She digested that she was actually going to be hanging out
with what may be considered friends. *Okay… well, cool.*

"Honey…don't get me wrong…I enjoy your company. But
how is it…that you have so much… free time to visit me?"
Shelia sighed. *Ah, the deja vu of old ladies wondering why I have
no life.* She sighed, "I'm unemployed."

"I see…"

"I do have an interview, though… so hopefully that will
work out…" Shelia trailed off. Miss Moon didn't say
anything.

Shelia played with her fingers. "So… uh… what do you do
for fun?" Shelia asked, cringing as soon as she asked it. (What
came to mind was how annoyed she was when Dipon asked
her that on their ill-fated date.)

Miss Moon blinked. "Sometimes the…caregivers take us out
for walks…or play bridge with us. Watch TV," Miss Moon
said monotonously.

"Ah…" *Damn, that is depressing.*

"Life is terrible when you're old, dear," Miss Moon said,
seeming to read Shelia's mind. Miss Moon's bluntness took
Shelia aback.

"I mean… really?" Shelia asked. She hadn't thought much
about her own life in the future, but suddenly the picture
looked bleak. "I don't know," she said. "The times I visited

my grandparents in China, they didn't seem that miserable to me?"

"Good…for them."

Christ. Shelia processed the fact that she was dealing with someone who was even more jaded than she was.

"C'mon, Miss Moon. The only reason you're so depressed is because you have nothing to do and no one to hang out with."

Miss Moon sighed. "I suppose…you're right. Is that why… you're here, then? Pity for an old woman?"

"No, no, it's not pity," Shelia said hastily. *Was it pity?* Miss Moon looked at her skeptically.

"It's because… I'm in the same boat as you," Shelia admitted, not realizing that was the case until she said it aloud.

"You're far too…young for that, dear," Miss Moon said.

"Um… well… I guess I'm trying to fix the situation. You could argue that it's not too late to fix yours, either."

Miss Moon just gave her a sad smile. "I'm the definition of… too late, dear."

Shelia rolled her eyes instinctively. "So, what—you're just going to wait until you die?"

Miss Moon looked at Shelia like she was mildly stupid. "That is what…folks like me are in here for, yes."

"No, that's a hospice. You're in here because you're supposed to live out the rest of your days in peace and harmony and all that, for god's sake."

"That's a…nice thought. A little naïve, but nice."
Shelia exhaled. She got up and grabbed the nearest pen and
paper, exasperated.

"Okay, Miss Moon," Shelia said, agitated. "You are going
to say what you would say to your kid, and I am going to
write it down for you."
Miss Moon stared at her in response. Shelia wasn't impressed
with her apparent stubbornness, but she changed her tone
anyway. "Come on. Right now, your family is all you have, so
you need to keep in touch with them. Remember how happy
you were when you got back that letter?"
Miss Moon frowned. "It's not that simple…"

"Maybe you're making it too complicated!" Shelia said,
annoyed. "Whatever—you know what, I'm just gonna start it.
Dear… whatever your daughter's name was…" Shelia said,
as she scrawled.

"Candace. Her name is…Candace," Miss Moon piped up.
Shelia took this as an encouraging sign. "Alright, dear…
Candace," Shelia wrote, looking to Miss Moon expectantly.
Miss Moon hesitated before saying, "Write…write that it is
wonderful to hear…that Kelsey and John are doing well.
Send them…my love. Has Richard gotten a job yet?
Everything here is…fine. The food is terrible, as always."
Shelia waited for Miss Moon to continue. Miss Moon looked
at her and said, "That's it."

"What? That's it?"

"Yes," Miss Moon said calmly.

This is probably the real reason Candace stopped writing, Shelia thought, sighing. *This letter is going to accomplish nothing. We should just...* Shelia thought with dawning realization, *call her damn grown kid. Duh.*

"Hey Moon," Shelia said. "Do you know Candace's number?"

"Candace's number...Ah, it always escapes me... So the nurses...taped it onto my drawer over there..."
Shelia located the number and punched it into her phone. "When was the last time you talked to Candace?"

"Oh dear... Perhaps I hadn't talked to her...in two months or so..."
Well, that's a little long for someone who has nobody else. "Okay, well, you're about to talk to her now," Shelia said, handing Miss Moon the phone as it rang. "I mean, if she's home or whatever."

"Hello?" a voice said through the speaker.

"Hello Candace... It's your mother speaking..."

"Oh," Candace's voice said, muffled through the phone. "How are you, Mom?"

"I'm the same as usual," Miss Moon said despondently. Her voice picked up when she asked, "How are you, dear?... How are the kids? Has Richard found a job yet?...How is your job? Have you eaten?"

"Oh... I'm fine," Candace replied, seeming overwhelmed at all the questions. "Richard is still looking... The job is going well… The kids are great… Oh, would you like to speak to them?" she added hastily. "They're just here watching T.V." In the background, Shelia heard faint protestations from the kids and Candace coaxing them to speak to their grandmother.

"Hi Grandma," one of the kids said reluctantly.

"Hello Katie," Miss Moon said with a wide smile. "How are you?"

"Good…" Katie in her distinctly five year-old voice said, clearly bored.

The painfully awkward conversation that was currently happening had Shelia recall the conversations she would have with her grandparents—the ones that never went beyond *"How are you?" "Good. How are you?" "Good."*

Katie didn't even try not to be audible when she said, "Mama, can I go back to watching Princess Kung-Fu now??"

"No, Katie, talk to your—"

"It's alright, Candace," Miss Moon said gently. "Let her watch…Princess what-now."

"Are you sure, Mom?"

"Yes, dear. I don't want her…to resent me for taking her away… from her favourite programme," Miss Moon said wryly. After exchanging a couple of more words, they said their goodbyes and hung up.

Shelia wasn't sure Miss Moon's conversation with her family had gone as successfully as she'd hoped.

"You're really not upset that your granddaughter doesn't want to talk to you?" Shelia asked, skeptical. *And your daughter, apparently… I guess this is the rocky relationship coming through.*

"She's five," Miss Moon said with a raised eyebrow. "It's not…personal. Hopefully when she gets older…she'll feel differently."

Shelia felt a pang of guilt. Maybe Miss Moon sensed it, or maybe it was just a coincidence when she asked, "How is your… relationship with your grandparents, dear?"

Shelia shrugged. "They live all the way over in China. The ones who are alive, anyway. Phone calls don't really do much…" Shelia suspected those calls would have been more meaningful were it not for the language barrier. *Old-person Mandarin is a different beast altogether… and my grandparents probably had trouble with my first-generation affectations, too.*

"So… it's nice when I get to see them, but it's not enough to really know who they are."

"I see…" Miss Moon said. "And your parents?"

So it's time to get to know my life story, huh?

"Well," Shelia started uncomfortably, "they did their best to provide for me, help me have a good life here. In return, I tried to make them happy, and proud of me, and all that…" *A little ironic that I'm now unemployed. And I still haven't told them.* A little bubble of shame cropped up within her.

"Did you…make them happy…at the expense of your own happiness?"

Shelia was caught off-guard. "Uh…I—no, I mean, well, I was happy to make them happy," Shelia stammered. As she said it, she had to question whether that was true. *Honestly… maybe it is and it isn't.*

"And… besides, you know, if I had done things solely for myself—well, I don't even know what that would look like, and even if I did, I still might be in as bad a shape, but without the support of my family, too, and really, who's to say one is better than the other, and…"
Shelia looked to Miss Moon, suddenly embarrassed at her word vomit. "Anyway, that's not really an appropriate question," she said defensively.

"I'm sorry, dear…I didn't mean to pry. I only…" Miss Moon searched for the words. She shook her head, giving up on the search. "Would you like to play some crib?" she asked, switching gears.
After a moment of deliberation, Shelia agreed. "Sure."
They played in silence. After a couple of rounds, Miss Moon broke the silence by saying, "You just remind me…so much like…myself. I'm a little bit worried for you," Miss Moon said.

"Ah," Shelia said. She didn't like appearing to be someone to be worry about, but she went along with it. "Well… what would you tell your twenty-seven year old self, then?"
Miss Moon didn't immediately answer the question. "Do you have children, Shelia? Or ever thought…about having them?"

"No… babysitting my friends' kids made me want to shoot myself, so I figured it's not really my thing," Shelia joked. Her tone became more serious when she added, "But… I mean, that realization was rather depressing."

"Depressing? I only wish… I'd had that realization myself," Miss Moon said.

Shelia took a moment to process what Miss Moon just said. "Are you saying you regret having children?" Shelia said, shocked.

"Maybe I don't regret having children, per se. I regret just falling into everything that was expected of me. Times were different then, of course…

"I was going steady with a boy long enough…that it made sense to get married. And after marriage…kids aren't a question…you simply expect that you will have them."

"With Candace, my eldest…the labour was very long and painful. It was done at the hospital. When it came time to the actual birth…they put me under anesthesia… twilight sleep. All I remember was hallucinating…and fighting to be conscious. It was frightening.

"When I woke up…Candace was handed to me. I was expecting a rush of warm maternal feelings. But all I felt like was…that there was an alien thing on me…that was vulnerable and helpless and… utterly dependent on me…and I could not go back. I was ashamed of feeling that way.

"I assumed the alien feeling would go away quickly…but it did not. And I found the work of motherhood itself so tedious…and unsatisfying. Walter was working long hours those days. Not that he'd be expected to help…I was grateful that my mother assisted me. But I don't know if she could relate to how I felt. It would be several agonizing months where…I wondered what in the world was wrong with myself.

"After close to a year…a personality started to emerge from my baby. I was astonished at this new light I saw her in…and the warmth and love I felt for her. It was a relief…to at last feel normal maternal feelings. But the other feeling of finding motherhood tedious…" she sighed. "That more or less stayed present throughout. With Candace, and with my second child, Liam. It coexisted with my love for my children.

"I did not have any language…nor framework for this dissatisfaction. I assumed it was simply life.

"In many ways…things got easier as they got older. But when Candace in particular became a young woman… society, by then…was drastically different from when I was the same age. There was all this possibility she had…that I never did. There's a certain shock that comes with realizing that…one's dissatisfaction didn't have to be so. A sense of all that time, wasted.

"I was happy for her, however…I realize now…I must have also been resentful. I didn't realize my resentment was about…all the world around me duping me about how life should be, not at her. But I'm afraid…my resentment may have leaked out…and used Candace as the target." Miss Moon closed her eyes, exhaling.

Shelia waited for Miss Moon to continue, and when she didn't, Shelia said, "That sounds rough, Moon. It sounds difficult for everyone involved."

"What can…be done about it now?" Miss Moon sighed. "Although…it is nice to be able to talk about this. I could never do that before…"

"Well, sure, it's good to get things off your chest. But you could always, you know, just talk to Candace about this. Explain where you were coming from back then."

Miss Moon frowned at the idea, dismissing it with a frail wave of the hand. "Can you do me a favour, dear?"

Sure, just reject my great idea and change the subject. "Sure," Shelia said, resigned.

"Can you read me a passage of that book over there, 'Tales of Munsch'? It's so hard for me to read these days…"

"Okay." Shelia picked up the book, flipping it open. " '*It was a quiet afternoon at the Worcestershire property…*' " she started.

"Sheliaaaaaaaaaaaaaa," Jeremiah said grandly, getting up from his seat. Shelia grinned despite herself. "Hey," she said, giving him a light hug. She took in the bar: it was going for a British dive look—wood panelling painted black, grimy mirrors, dim lighting—without actually being dive. Shelia herself didn't approve of dingyness-as-aesthethic, but *hey, at least I was invited.*

She spotted Elizabeth next, greeting her with a "Heyy," as well. She proceeded to stress over whether she should give Elizabeth a hug too—*I don't know her as well as Jeremiah but not hugging makes our formality awkward and obvious so I'm not really sure what to—*

"Hey!" Elizabeth said enthusiastically, going for the hug herself. "How are you?"

"Uh," Shelia said as she pulled away, "You know, things. Good," she said, cringing as soon as she said it. *God, I guess my social skills are rusty. I'm gonna need to get me some alcohol as social lubricant…*

"Guys, this is Shelia, an old coworker of mine," Jeremiah said to his entourage.

"Hi," Shelia said, surveying the table. In addition to Elizabeth and Jeremiah, there were three other people: two white guys and a brown guy.

"Oh, fuck," Shelia said, realizing the brown guy was Dipon. *Crap, I just said that out loud. Gotta improvise something…* she thought at the quizzical looks of those at the table.

"Ah, sorry—just stubbed my toe," Shelia said hastily. "Instead of saying 'ow' like normal people, I swear like a sailor," she laughed breezily, hoping her face wasn't going red.

"Oh, I'm sure that's the reason," Dipon said.

God, this motherfucker, Shelia thought. She decided to take the bait. "Ah, yes, what other reason could there possibly be for such an outburst?"

The group was silent. Dipon looked gleeful that the bait had been taken. Before Dipon could respond a blond football type piped up and said, "Hey Shelia, I'm Brad. I'm Liz's brother— Dipon and I are dating."

Shelia smiled amicably in response, thankful for the return to peaceful social territory. *Ah, interracial and gay,* Shelia thought. *I probably shouldn't be making a big deal out of it, even in my head… but with a football dude, no less!*

The remaining unidentified person, a skinny white guy with curly hair, nodded. "Hey—Vince. Jeremiah and I go way back as drinking buddies." Shelia gave a friendly nod back.

While everyone was introducing themselves, Jeremiah was regarding Dipon and Shelia, amused. Finally, he said, "So, you guys already know each other, eh?"

Damnit, why can't you ignore uncomfortable things and let peaceful social interactions be peaceful? Shelia thought, communicating as much in a dirty look towards Jeremiah. He smiled, sly, in return.

Dipon looked to Shelia to answer. After hesitation on her part, she finally said, "Well—I guess we went on a blind date, but it actually wasn't a date. And then Dipon decided to critique my social skills."

"Dipon!" Brad chastised good-naturedly.

"Hey, hey, I did it nicely," Dipon said, holding his hands up.

"Ohohohoho," Jeremiah said. "Somehow, that makes perfect sense for both of you," Jeremiah said, entertained.

"Dipon, I guess you didn't realize who you were dealing with."

"No, I did not," Dipon chuckled.

"God, you guys are such assholes," Shelia said, rolling her eyes. She found that it was actually nice to be rid of peaceful social interaction and go straight into trash talk, but she hoped her (lack of) social skills wouldn't be the topic at hand for much longer. "Isn't it a sign of poor social skills to critique someone else's social skills the moment you meet them, anyway?"

"That's a fair point," Elizabeth said.

"In my personal experience, I prefer people pointing things out to me! How else are you gonna figure out your blind spots, y'know what I'm saying?" Dipon said.

"Dude, you gotta learn that Shelia's mannerisms are part of her charm," Jeremiah said, winking at Shelia. "That sarcastic, abrasive character is gold."

"Gee, thanks. That's the first time anyone has described me as remotely charming."

Dipon said, "Hey, I agree," with a jokester smile. "To Shelia's charming, abrasive nature," he said, raising his glass. They clinked, and Shelia did not get the sense that she was the butt of a joke.

"Aw… you guys are friends now," Vince teased in a baby voice.

"That's more friends than you have," Dipon grinned.

"Ohhhhhhhh," Jeremiah said, as Vince mimicked being shot in the heart.

Towards the end of the night, Shelia considered whether she should go home with Vince. *God, it's been a while since I've had sex...* On the other hand, she felt rather neutral about him in terms of attraction. She sensed that he felt the same. *And I'm not a fan of implied pair-the-spares, anyway.*

"It was nice to meet everyone. I had a good time. Thanks for inviting me, Jeremiah," she said, ready to leave.

"We do this thing every Monday. Feel free to stop by next week," Jeremiah said amicably.

"Yeah, for sure," the others echoed in agreement.

Shelia smiled, basking in the social acceptance. "Oh, okay, alright. Well then... see you guys," she waved.

"This doesn't make any sense," Monica said.

"Yeah. I'm confused," Justin said, eyebrows furrowed.

Shelia sighed. Shelia was trying to explain to the kids how Boolean expressions with 'if, then' statements worked. She resisted the urge to say, impatiently, "What don't you get?!" *Don't do that. That would be a bad call, bad call...*

"Okay," she said instead, "remember when I said that computers are like very pedantic toddlers? That you have to be extremely specific when you want something done, or they get super confused?"

They nodded.

"Let me illustrate with an analogy about…" Shelia thought, looking around. "Pasta," she said, adding quickly, "Uh, you guys have made pasta before?"

Justin shrugged. "Noodles are like pasta, right?"

"Uh, I guess they are," Shelia said off-handedly. "So… if you were to make pasta, what's the first thing you'd do?

"Uh, boil it," Monica said, in a *duh* tone.

"Ah, see, you're getting ahead of yourself, Monica," Shelia said. "Remember, computers are toddlers that don't know anything unless you tell them. What do you do before you boil the pasta?"

"Boil the water?" Justin said.

Shelia nodded encouragingly, "And before that?"

"Fill the pot, turn on the heat…" Monica said.

"Yep," Shelia said. "So, so far, we have 'fill the pot with water', then 'turn on the heat', and then 'wait for it to boil'. In Boolean terms, we could say if 'having a pot = true', then proceed to fill the pot say, 3/4 full. Then we could say, if the 'pot is filled with water = true', then put it on the stove. If 'pot is on stove = true', then turn the heat on high—get the gist?" Monica nodded slowly.

"What about when it's not true?" Justin asked.

"Good question. Let's try adding a false scenario with the next part: the pasta. Monica, want to give the first 'if, then' statement a shot?"

"Um, okay," Monica said, thinking about it. "If… 'having pasta = true', then open the packet."

"Uh-huh," Shelia nodded encouragingly. "Okay, Justin—if it's false?"

"Uhhhhhhhhh," he said. "If having pasta is false… then go buy some pasta?"

Shelia and Monica chuckled. "Yes, you've got it. Now, the whole 'go buy pasta' thing is a whole 'nother rabbit hole, so we'll skip it— but Monica, if the 'packet is open = true', then what?"

"Then pour it in the pot."

"Nice. There's another thing though—we want to make sure it's not any old pot. It has to be the pot on the stove with the water. So, we can specify, if the packet is open, the pot is filled, the pot is on the stove, and the heat is on ALL equal true, then we can go ahead and pour the pasta in."

"Oh… shit, that's a lot."

In a weary *been-there* tone she said, "Yeah… it can get very complicated very quickly. So, if 'pasta is in the pot = true'…?" Shelia trailed off, leaving the kids to fill in the blanks.

"Then… then take the pot and pour it into a sieve," Justin said.

"Okay—but what if it's not cooked?" Shelia asked.

"If 'pasta is in the pot = true' and 'pasta is cooked = true', then pour it into the strainer," Monica corrected.

"And if 'pasta is in the pot = true' and 'pasta is cooked = false', then wait until it's true to pour it into the strainer," Justin finished.

Shelia looked over her pupils approvingly. "I'm impressed. You guys got the hang of it quickly."

Monica punched Justin's shoulder. "Yo, we did it."

"Okay... but what does "if, then" shit have to do with video games?" Justin asked.

"You'll see now," Shelia said, opening the editor for them. "Video games have to have statements in them like, 'if player one gets hit by a slime monster = true', then decrease their HP by 3 points."

"Oh, I gotcha."

"So, what we're gonna do here is use 'if, then' statements with moving pixels..." Shelia explained the exercise to them, and then stood back while they tinkered with the code.

"So, Shelia," Monica said when they were packing up. "My mom's kind of suspicious of you, so she invited you for dinner. Will you come?"

"I'mma be there too," Justin added.

"Oh," Shelia said, taken aback. *Eh, I can see where her mom is coming from, I guess I am a random person who has taken it upon herself to teach these kids coding.* "Uh... sure."

"Sweeet," Monica said.

"Oh Shelia, are you coming to Yoyo's closing party?" Justin asked.

"You have to come, Shelia," Monica insisted.

"Oh, um…" Shelia said, taken by surprise again. "I forgot about that…" It was three weeks from today. She was still pissed at Yoyo for kicking her out. And she didn't accept that Yoyo's Books should go down without a fight. *But if I don't go, that might be the last time I'll see Yoyo's Books.* "We'll see, okay?" she said firmly.

"But—"

"We'll see," Shelia insisted. "Catch you guys next week."

"See you!"

"Bye," Monica said. "Come to the party!!"

Shelia shut the door, smiling.

"You know, I've… never asked you… but have you got a fella, dear?"

"No," Shelia replied while staring intently at the crib board. She moved the small blue peg four dots forward. She waited for Miss Moon to make her move, but Miss Moon herself was waiting for Shelia to elaborate.

Shelia looked at her. "I don't know what to tell you. I had one very long-term relationship, and afterwards a series of casual hook—," she paused. "er, a series of casual beaus…"

"I'm not blind to…how you young folk like to sleep around, you know."

"Ah… well, not all of us have the constitution of a monk."

Miss Moon gave her a lightly disapproving look in response. *Whatever, she's from a different era.* "Anyway. That's all I have to say about my love life."

Miss Moon looked at her for a moment. Shelia resisted the urge to squirm under her scrutiny. "Loose behaviour aside," Miss Moon finally said, "I think you should relish your time being single."

"Right," Shelia said, "use the time to 'find myself'."

"You don't even realize…" Miss Moon trailed off, shaking her head. "You're of a different generation, I suppose. I myself was…married when I was eighteen, as I discussed before."

"Um… right," Shelia said, suddenly feeling bad about waving her *single-independent-woman* status in Miss Moon's face.

"I was fifty-five when Liam, the youngest, moved out. My husband and I…" Miss Moon frowned. "We'd been growing apart since we got married. But the children…provided an excuse to ignore the rift…"

"And once the kids moved out, you couldn't ignore the rift anymore," Shelia stated.

"Oh, yes, I could," she said. "I could've ignored it…like my life depended on it. In a way, it had…because I was completely unknown to myself…with my children and my husband gone." Miss Moon's face reflected a deep sadness. "Of course…Walter couldn't ignore it. I pleaded with him to reconsider. To try...and work things out. But he wouldn't listen."

Shelia was alarmed at the watery twinkle in Moon's eye. She continued, "He went off to sail the world like he'd always dreamed of doing, once the divorce was done with. I got some money from the settlement, but I had to get a job at the grocery store. Can you imagine, at nearly sixty, working at the grocery store!" Miss Moon shook her head with a slight smile.

"The married friends I'd had...lost touch after my divorce. They were mostly Walter's friends and their wives. They would've scoffed...looking at me working at the grocery store."

"That time was hard on my pride," she admitted, "but at the same time...I was proud of myself for doing it on my own. I made new, much younger, friends, I was moving on. I was learning about who I was."

"Well, that sounds good," Shelia said hesitantly, knowing there was a catch.

"Yes...it was." Miss Moon frowned. "But one day, as I was preparing for a shift...as you might guess," she chuckled ruefully, "I fell and broke my hip. I yelled for help so maybe neighbours could come over, but they didn't hear me... so I was just lying there...

"A coworker, Jillian...she was such a pretty and nice girl... noticed that I hadn't shown up to my shift. She called me... and when I didn't answer, she suspected the situation I was in, and got an off-duty coworker to come check on me. When he reached my apartment…it was Nick, a rather nice fellow… he heard me yelling in pain through the door."

Miss Moon sighed. "After that incident, my children convinced me that I should move to assisted living, for my own safety. I agreed with them," she said flatly. "And so… here I am." Miss Moon finished. Shelia nodded slowly, not sure what to make of the story yet.

"Oh, look at me, prattling on about my life," Miss Moon waved. "I just meant to say…young women of today are so lucky that they have so much choice. That other things can come to mind…in the first place. I want you to feel that." Shelia nodded solemnly. "So…" she said, "what other things would you have liked to come to mind?"

"Oh, I…I don't know!" she laughed, and in her condition, it was more of a cough-laugh. "I always liked baking, so perhaps a bake-shop…and…Prague. I've always wanted to visit Prague…" she said. "But that's in the past…no use thinking of it now…"

Looking at Miss Moon's wistful face, Shelia thought she should try to get her mind off the subject of unfulfilled hopes and dreams.

"It's still your turn, Moon," Shelia said, nodding towards the crib board.

"Oh," Moon said, moving her peg forward.

Shelia moved her peg forward as well. *So, Moon is basically going to stew in her misery until she kicks the bucket,* Shelia frowned, thinking the same thought she had when she'd first met her.

Miss Moon was deliberating on her move. *The main reason she's sad is because she's lonely and bored…* Shelia recalled the 'Friends' chapter of 'A Practical Guide to Life'.

You have more friends than you think… They've just fallen by the wayside or haven't been given a chance to develop.

Eyeing the move Miss Moon just made, Shelia asked, "Were all of your friends from your married life really that judgemental? There must've been some that were sympathetic."

"Hmm… Beatrice was quite nice… we'd get along, you know… she'd always compliment my cooking skills…"

"Are you curious to see what she's up to nowadays?" Shelia prodded.

"Beatrice?" Miss Moon thought about it. "Yes, it would be interesting to hear about how she's doing…her and Jim too…" she mused. "Really, I'd like hear about how everyone is doing… But…it just hurt, that they didn't seek me out after the divorce…"

"Yeah, that's shitty," Shelia said. "They probably didn't do it on purpose. They were probably, you know, lazy." She moved her piece four spaces ahead. *Look at me, appointing myself as Moon's life coach—never thought I'd be taking hints from that damn book.*

"And your grocery buddies? Did you ever stay in touch with them?" Shelia asked further.

Miss Moon smiled. "Those young people…they actually did visit me in here once or twice, but you know, their lives are in such flux — moving, school, starting families…"

Shelia nodded. Moving towards her end goal for Miss Moon, she asked, "So, Moon… did you ever keep an address book, or anything like that?"

"Ah…yes…" Miss Moon said, skeptical. "Why? You're not going to call them…are you? I don't know about that…"

"I'm not going to. But I think you should," Shelia said gently. "I think they'd like hearing from you."

Miss Moon furrowed her eyebrows, and looked back and forth between Shelia and her dresser for a while.

Finally, Miss Moon lifted a slow finger. "My address book is in…that top drawer…over there," Miss Moon said, skepticism still in her voice. Shelia obligingly brought it over.

"Who…should I call?" Miss Moon asked, uncertain.

In that moment, Miss Moon's vulnerability struck Shelia. *This is kinda hard for her.*

She cleared her throat. "Beatrice? Or maybe the coworker who found you?… Or the one who called for help?" Shelia shrugged.

Miss Moon nodded. Shelia passed her the phone, and Miss Moon started dialling, hands shaky, clutching the phone tightly. Shelia heard the telltale voicemail beep, and Miss Moon hung up.

I wouldn't have left a voicemail, either, honestly. "Try another," Shelia prodded.

Miss Moon looked at Shelia uncertainly. Shelia tried to look as encouraging as possible.

Finally, Miss Moon dialled again. After a couple of seconds, Shelia heard a *"Hello?"*

Promisingly, it sounded like an older female voice.

"Oh, hi," Miss Moon said, seeming surprised that the phone picked up. "Er... this is Darlene Moon calling. Is Beatrice in... by any chance?"

Darlene's her real name, huh?

"Oh!" the speaker exclaimed. "Darlene! *What* a surprise! I would have never guessed I'd be hearing from you after all of this time."

"Beatrice, it's nice to hear from you," Miss Moon said warmly.

"Well, how are you Darl?" Beatrice asked.

"Oh, ah, I've been well..." Miss Moon said. "How about yourself? How is Andrew and your family?"

"Oh, we've been great," Beatrice said. "My youngest recently had twins," Beatrice said jubilantly.

"Oh, that's wonderful," Miss Moon said.

"How is your family?" Beatrice asked, genuinely curious. "Er... have you and Walter been in touch?"

"They're busy with raising their young families, you know," Miss Moon said. "And we've been in touch here and there," Miss Moon said stiffly.

"I see," Beatrice said, and Shelia could practically hear her nodding as she said that.

There was a pause in conversation. Beatrice eventually broke it, saying, "Darl, I've got to say… I'm sorry that we lost touch."

Miss Moon looked surprised to hear this. "Oh, Beatrice, you don't—"

"No, I do. Especially because there was no good reason for it, except maybe plain old laziness. I'm sorry. I'm glad you called… I've missed you."

Miss Moon looked to Shelia, gap-mouthed.

Wow. This call is going even better than I expected. Shelia gave Miss Moon a thumbs-up.

"Beatrice, you know… I could have called before too…"

"But you were probably in such distress, after your divorce. We should have been there for you."

Miss Moon blinked, taking it in. "You know…it's okay…it's in the past," she said, almost as if to convince herself.

There was a pause before Beatrice responded. "I still want to make up for that lost time, and reconnect. Can I call you again this Wednesday?"

"I'd love that."

After exchanging details and hanging up, Miss Moon handed the phone to Shelia shakily.

Shelia took it and said, "Look at you, reconnecting with your old pals."

Miss Moon gave her a rare smile, and they resumed their game of crib.

"Shelia, you're officially unbanished from Yoyo's," Monica announced through the buzzer, when Shelia answered the call.

"Uh, what?"

"It's been a month," Justin said, voice muffled through the intercom.

"Uh, okay, thanks for the PSA," Shelia said dryly. *Hm, I guess it has been a month.* "Anyway, come in, today we're gonna cover—"

"Shelia—let's do the lesson at Yoyo's," Justin urged.

"Yeah. Everybody there misses you and stuff," Monica added.

Shelia frowned. She weighed her options: *A) Refuse and have the lesson at my apartment as planned, and seem petty. B) Reveal myself as a sucker to these kids and go. C) Feign laziness for leaving the apartment. D) People actually miss me?*

"Okay, I'll go—for the homeless dudes," Shelia finally said.

"Yesssssss!"

"Come inside while I get my coat, it's freezing," she grumbled, pressing the front door button as it beeped.

Shelia took in the familiar surroundings: the death-and-taxes rubber chicken, the faded but colourful ambience, the used-books smell, the tinkly bell that announced their arrival.

"Heyyy, it's you!" one of the Yoyo's regulars exclaimed to Shelia.

"Hey, it's you," Shelia smiled back. (Evidently, neither of them knew each other's names.) *Maybe I should figure that out sometime.*

"Hey Yoyo," Monica waved.

"Shelia's gonna teach us how to make a video game here," Justin informed. He gently took Shelia's laptop and went to get seated towards the back of the store.

"Oh, is that so?" Yoyo asked.

Shelia looked at Yoyo for the first time in a month. She seemed to have aged disproportionately in that time.

"I'm here because they asked me to," Shelia said curtly.

"I see," Yoyo said.

Shelia promptly made her way towards the back, avoiding any more talk with Yoyo. She knew she'd have to discuss her resentment at some point, but she wasn't in the mood for it at the moment.

She found Monica and Justin at the usual hang out area at the back of the store, already preoccupied.

"Joel, you've got it down—just remember to close the tags," Monica explained, as he was tinkering on Shelia's laptop.

"Yeah, like that," Justin encouraged.

"So…" Shelia said, joining her pupils, "we ready for the next lesson?"

The lesson took longer than Shelia anticipated, because five more students joined them over the course of her teaching—two looked like the 2 am homeless dudes, one was another youth, and the last, a middle-class adult. But Shelia didn't mind the extra students. And Monica and Justin helped her out when they could, anyway.

"Remember the quotation marks, dude!" Justin said.

"Try to keep in mind the mechanics of the code, rather than copy and pasting, once you get the hang of it," Shelia noted.

"Cloooooose your tags, y'all," Monica reminded everybody. The progress was slow-going, but at least there was some progress.

"This seems crazy complicated," the youth, a boy named Len, said. "Can all of this coding really turn into that?" he asked, nodding towards the video game station in the corner.

"It can," Shelia said. "It is a long way of going from what we're doing to that, but, y'know, baby steps."

"This stuff is tricky," said Joel. "But it'd be neat to see the end result."

At the close of the lesson, Shelia remarked, "It'd be nice if we had more than one laptop." As she put her laptop in its case, she said, "Good job everybody. I'll see you… uh, when I see you, I guess."

The group did not seem satisfied with Shelia's vague plans. Joel inquired, "When is the next lesson?"

"Uhhh…" she said, as others expectantly waited for her answer. "Let's say Tuesday at five," she decided, at random.

"Nice. I'll catch you then," he nodded.

"Bye," the others echoed.

"See you next week, Mrs. Teacher," Justin grinned.

"Don't call me that, Justin," Shelia admonished, on cue.
Who would have thought I'd be here, teaching the homeless and random people coding?
She watched the coders go, leaving just her and Yoyo in the store. *Should I voice my resentment to Yoyo, or should I just leave?* The two women looked at each other. Yoyo, expectantly; Shelia, inscrutably.

"You're upset with me," Yoyo said.
Well. Less likely that I'm just gonna leave now. She crossed her arms. "Yeah. I still don't agree with your decision to banish me."
She braced herself for some bullshit reasoning from Yoyo—she wasn't gonna have any of it.

"I agree with you, Shelia. It wasn't the right call."
What?
"Uh… really?" she asked, raising her eyebrows.

"Yes. In my head, I was doing the right thing for you, but what I was really doin' was providing an excuse… for you not to see me in this state a' mine. I knew I had become this, guru figure or whatever to you, and I didn't want you to see me as less-than. This whole closing down again thing has got me a little unhinged."
Shelia processed this new information, her mind spinning. She was not expecting Yoyo to talk about feeling 'less-than.'

"Uh… so… what made you realize that?"

"Oh, I don't know, how I was goin' and avoidin' people in general," Yoyo responded. "Sayin' I was fine instead of being

175

honest. Thinking about what ya said, about how friends don't ban each other from their establishments and all... it made me think, prob'ly banning you wasn't about you. It was more so about me feelin' triggered from, once again, facing the onslaught of the colonial society."

Shelia nodded slowly, taking it in. Finally, she relaxed, the last of her indignant feelings giving way.

"For god's sake, Yoyo," Shelia said, exasperated, "if the thought of shutting down stresses you out so much, why aren't you fighting to keep Yoyo's open?"

Yoyo sighed. "I get that perseverin' spirit, but you don't understand—Yoyo's has been pulled from the brink twice already. I don't know, what if it's a sign that it's... just not meant to be," Yoyo said, sadness permeating her face.

"Bullshit," Shelia said immediately. "Yoyo, you started with literally nothing," she said, indicating grandly to the space around her, "and you built this. If it's been revived twice, that means people care about this damn place enough to revive it two freakin' times! Most importantly, you don't want it to close. I mean..." Shelia paused. She slowed her roll and stopped to consider: Yoyo was old. Running a small business, and an independent book store at that, is a stressful endeavour. *Does she want to move on? Does she want to retire in the countryside with her family, and be a pillar there instead of here? Have I just been selfish in wanting to keep Yoyo's open, without considering what Yoyo wants?* "You don't want it to close, right?"

Yoyo shook her head. "No, I don't," she murmured. "Sure, my life might be easier if I let it close and go back to the country. But I don't feel done here yet. I still got work to do here."

Shelia nodded. "Then we'll fight to keep it open," she said simply.

Yoyo smiled briefly. "Shelia, thank you," she said, putting a hand on Shelia's shoulder. "For your faith in this ol' thing. I don't know if I'll regret having you sway me," Yoyo smirked, "but I think I will fight for this thing."

"Tell people that the closing party is now a fundraising party," Shelia said with bravado.

7

Shelia found herself back at 117 street and Bellevue, in Olivia's perfectly-decorated quaint house, for Olivia's 'How to Spring Back from Getting Your Ass Fired' sessions.

As usual, Olivia had a spread straight out of a food magazine, which Shelia was diligently snacking on. Shelia noted how the vibe of the group had gone from support for tech people to a general get-together.

"Hey Shelia!" Amber greeted, while Shelia was chewing. Shelia quickly gulped down her food, responding, "Oh, hey Amber."

Amber took the liberty of pulling out the intricate wooden chair beside Shelia, and took a seat. "A couple of my friends took a look at my new website and loved it, so I gave them your contact info. I hope you don't mind."

"Oh," Shelia said, surprised. "Of course I don't mind. Thanks for the reference."

"No problem," Amber said. "You know, I tried looking for you online but didn't really find anything. I think you should consider promoting your services, Shelia."

"Uh… I hadn't thought of it. Thanks for the tip," she said, while thinking, *I have to PROMOTE myself? Ugh.*

"So… how goes the used bookstore?" Amber asked, sipping her wine.

Shelia chewed thoughtfully before replying, "My banishment period was up, so the kids made me go to Yoyo's for their usual coding lesson. Somehow, it turned into a group coding lesson and I ended up teaching some homeless guys and other people. It was a bit of a challenge because we had to split a laptop between seven people, but I think they learned something… maybe. And Yoyo and I sorted out our differences. And I ended up convincing her to try and keep Yoyo's open, via a fundraiser, instead of letting it close," she finished, going for another h'ors d'oeuvre but forcing herself to stop midway.

"Wow," Amber nodded. "You know, I was thinking—this 'Yoyo's bookstore' has a lot of intrigue behind it. We have the central person, Yoyo, who's overcome all this adversity to create this space that is so important to the community around it. I think it would make for a really strong story.

Would you be interested in having us come a cover one of your coding classes at Yoyo's, Shelia? It could be a great boost for getting people to the fundraiser."

"Seriously?" Shelia said. "That'd be awesome," she said, before she had a chance to panic at the thought of being on the news.

"I heard coding," Jeremiah popped by, inserting himself into the conversation. "What's up?" Elizabeth, Vince, and Olivia were with him, too.

"Hey Shelia," Elizabeth smiled. Vince gave her a friendly nod.

"Shelia's nobly teaching coding to the downtrodden, and I'm covering it for a story," Amber filled them in.

"Shelia," Olivia said, impressed, "I didn't know you had a philanthropic streak."

Shelia's mind rejected this description immediately. "Um, no, it just kind of happened randomly—"

"That sounds great, Shelia," Elizabeth interrupted. "Let me know when you're doing the next coding sesh, I'd love to help out."

"That way you'd have more than one laptop for seven people," Amber pointed out.

"Oh, I'd be happy to lend mine for the cause," Jeremiah said.

"Me too," Olivia added.

Okay. Wow. This is becoming a thing. "Oh, wow... thanks guys. So, all you really need to do is download a software editor..."

While Shelia explained the logistics of the plan, Brandon said to Olivia, "Hey Livvy, I have to get going now," placing a light hand on her waist. He waited for Shelia to finish her spiel before telling everyone, "Have fun. Nice seeing you all."

"Bye babe, thanks for your help setting up," Olivia responded with a quick kiss, as the rest of the group bid him goodbye.

Huh. Olivia's beau in person. Together their combined good-lookingness is blinding. She shook off her mere-mortal feelings and made her rounds talking with everyone, as the living room slowly filled.

Wow, I'm like, socializing, she thought. She ended up in a conversation with Olivia and someone Shelia didn't know. The mystery person gushed, "Olivia, I've always loved your get-togethers. You have a real knack for hosting and bringing people together."

Olivia put a hand on her heart. "Aw, thanks, Nagini, I appreciate it." Shelia's first instinct was to snark internally about this display of sentimentality, but she resisted. *I actually… agree that Olivia's events are nice. Especially the food.*

"Nagini, this is Shelia, by the way," Olivia said. "She was my coworker. She's a real firestarter."

"Ah, Olivia, you flatter me…" Shelia said, shaking Nagini's hand.

"Nice to meet you," Nagini said warmly. "Olivia, I'm so sorry I didn't make it out to your last thing. I unexpectedly got sick," she said apologetically.

"Oh, girl, no worries!" Olivia said, waving away the apology. "I'm glad you're feeling better and could make it today."

"Actually," Nagini said sheepishly, "I might not be better for another nine months…"

When it dawned on Olivia, she shrieked, "Oh my god! Nagini! You're pregnant?!" At Olivia's outburst, the guests surrounding them gave curious looks.

"Did I hear a pregnancy?!" Lily shrieked.

Nagini nodded enthusiastically, grinning. "Yep. I'm pregnant, everyone!"

The room cheered, and those who had drinks in hand toasted her.

"Oh, congratulations, Gini," Olivia said, giving Nagini a bear hug.

"Congrats," Shelia said as well, partly because she felt she was supposed to and partly because of Nagini's genuine-seeming joy.

Shelia noted Olivia's slightly watery eyes when Olivia pulled away. *Damn. She really feels for her friends.* Shelia felt a twinge of jealousy that other people had such close relationships and she didn't.

She was starting to feel like an awkward interloper intruding upon a grand friendship, so she schemed about how to exit the conversation. *I could probably just leave, they wouldn't notice anyway. Or the solid bathroom excuse…*

It turns out, Shelia didn't need to do anything. "I'll be right back," Olivia excused herself, placing a hand on Shelia's shoulder.

Shelia and Nagini's current party of two quickly expanded, with people coming in either to congratulate Nagini or inquire about the pregnancy.

Despite knowing she didn't want kids, Shelia didn't mind the talk of babies. Shelia found the window into the foreign world slightly intriguing.

"How far along are you?

"Six weeks today!"

"Wow, you're hardly showing...."

But finding that she legitimately had to pee, Shelia excused herself, cutting her visit to the baby world short.

She wandered out of the buzzing living room into the comparatively quiet hallway. She admired the Persian rug lining the floor, as she always did when she came to Olivia's house.

As the location of the bathroom was not obvious, Shelia methodically opened each door—*Nope, nope, not tha—*

"Oh! Hey Olivia, sorry, was just looking for the…" Shelia stopped short, noting Olivia's red nose, "…bathroom…"

"Oh," Olivia said, looking shocked. "It's two doors to the left," Olivia said, giving a teary smile.

Shelia nodded slowly, her mind reeling. She had no idea what to do. She had minimal experience consoling people and was also not very good at it.

"Uh…Olivia…what's wrong?" Shelia asked, cautiously. Olivia waved her off, giving her another smile. "It's okay, I'm okay. I'm sorry for all of…this," she indicated to her tear-stained face, rolling her eyes. "I'll just be out in a bit."

"Um…okay…" Shelia said uncertainly. She started to turn away, but stopped. "Olivia. You know… you don't have to say anything if you don't want to. But you don't have to force yourself to go back out there and be the perfect hostess. Take your time. We'll survive," Shelia smirked.

Olivia smiled briefly, and it wasn't an *I'm-actually-fine!* smile this time. "Thanks, Shelia."

Shelia nodded, turning away. She processed what had just transpired. *It's silly, but… I thought she was immune to sadness.* When Olivia did return to the party, Shelia tried to give her space. When they caught each other's eye, Olivia gave her a knowing smile. *Damn. If I were in her position, I'd have never left my room.*

One person left the get-together, which then triggered a domino effect of everyone leaving.

"Shelia, I look forward to the group coding lesson," Jeremiah said heartily, as he and Elizabeth put on their coats.

"Me too. Good on you, Shelia, for setting that up," Elizabeth said.

"Well, thanks for offering to help out," Shelia said, as she buttoned her coat.

They hugged Olivia goodbye, and closed the door behind them with Olivia waving.

Shelia was about to follow them out the door when Olivia asked, "Hey Shelia, before you take off, can I talk to you?"

"Uh—yeah, what's up?" Shelia asked mid-button, apprehensive.

"So, it was probably obvious why I was upset," Olivia said sheepishly. "But the reason was… You know, we've been trying for over two years now? I was so excited when I finally got pregnant this year… but it ended in a miscarriage. It was pretty early, before we'd told anyone…"

"I'm sorry to hear that, Olivia," Shelia said. Shelia couldn't relate to Olivia's problem, but she did sympathize with her sadness.

"Yeah… I still feel raw from the grief, honestly," Olivia said. "And I feel like I'm at the peak with my frustration with all of this, with my uterus, with the tracking and the peeing on sticks and how with all of my friends every freaking time they fuck a kid pops out," she said in one breath, "and I just couldn't handle Nagini's announcement at the moment." A look of realization came to Olivia's face when she said, "Oh, Shelia, I'm sorry, I didn't mean to dump this all on you. It's probably so boring to you, anyway… I never thought I'd be one of those fertility-obsessed women, God… but it kind of sneaks up on you," Olivia said. She regained her composure. "Anyway, I just wanted to let you know, so you don't think that I don't trust you enough to tell you."

Shelia felt oddly honoured that Olivia would want to tell her this. "It's okay, Olivia. I understand, you need to be able to bitch about it."

Olivia laughed, relieved at Shelia's response. "Yeah. Bitching is nice," she concurred.

"Shelia… do you ever feel weird, now that we're at that age where all of our friends are making little versions of themselves? I mean… are *you* secretly pregnant right now?"

Shelia paused. She sheepishly said, "Uh, well, actually—"

Olivia's eyes widened, and her hands flew to her mouth.

After a pause, Shelia burst out laughing. Probably harder than was warranted, but she suspected it was due to all her years of unused laughter coming out.

Mock-scandalized, Olivia exclaimed, "Oh my god, you little trickster!"

She cracked up, too.

When they both calmed down, Shelia clarified, "So, I'm not gonna be pregnant any time soon, or ever."

"I respect that position, Shelia," Olivia said.

"As for feeling weird about all my friends getting pregnant…" Shelia continued. "Well, I don't have any friends in the first place to have that problem," she said, matter-of-factly.

Olivia frowned. "Oh, Shelia, that's not true."

"I know, I know, there's all the Cogville people like you… but there's a difference between work friends, and like, friend friends, you know?" She added, "But I don't know, lately... I feel like that gap is maybe getting bridged..."

Olivia considered Shelia's words. "Shelia, I'm glad to hear that. Whoever gets to be your *friend* friend is lucky."

"What?" Shelia said, her cognitive dissonance kicking in. "No, you know what I'm like..."

"Yeah, I do," Olivia challenged. "You're a sarcastic wisecracker who can't help but tell it like it is. You can't help but be yourself, even if you try not to be. Your authenticity is so *refreshing*, you have no idea. And—underneath all of that cynicism, you care deeply, Shelia."

Shelia blinked, not sure of what to say. She wondered if there was truth to what Olivia was saying. *Who knew that Olivia was so perceptive? Or at least, could come across as pretty damn perceptive?*

Either way, Shelia hadn't felt seen in a long time, and she was thankful. "Thanks, Olivia," she murmured.

Olivia gave a don't-mention-it nod. "So... you wanna do coffee sometime? Bridge that gap?"

"Yes," Shelia replied. "Definitely."

Shelia knocked uncertainly on door two-thirteen. She could smell food wafting through the room.

The door swung open, revealing a woman with deep crow's feet and a soft roundness to her. "Hello, you must be Shelia," the person greeted. "I'm Cheyenne, Monica's mom."

"Omigosh," Monica exclaimed, popping into view, "you made it!" She attack-hugged Shelia. Monica's bursts of affection had freaked out Shelia less and less these days, and so Shelia gave a proper hug back. "Yep… I survived the journey to get to your place. It's a miracle."

"Ah, you're a funny one," Cheyenne said. "Monica's told me a lot about you. Come take a seat." Cheyenne directed her towards the dining table, which took up a portion of the living room. During her short trek to the table, Shelia could see that it was a two-bedroom one-bathroom kind of deal, with a balcony that overlooked the street below. Some kids were running around the street, while cars passed intermittently.

The table was already almost half full when Shelia took her seat. Shelia could hear Cheyenne and Monica bustling in the kitchen.

"So you're the computer teacher," said a gap-toothed child that Shelia could only assume was a younger sister.

"No, she's a random person from Yoyo's," corrected a middle sibling sitting next to her.

"You are both right," Shelia noted.

A grandmotherly person spoke up and said, "It's nice to meet you, Shelia. I think you have been a very good influence on Monica." The woman looked like an older version of Cheyenne.

"Well, Monica is a pretty good kid to start with," Shelia responded. As usual, Shelia was uncomfortable with the flattery, but what she said about Monica was true.

Steaming basket of fried bread in hand, Monica announced, "I made this myself. Also, I heard my name."

"We were just talking about how much you stink," the middle sibling said.

"No, we were not," Grandma clarified.

"Monica, that looks crazy good," Shelia noted, ignoring the stink-talk. "Who knew you were secretly a great cook?"

"My Monica has always had a knack for it," her grandma said proudly.

"Thanks, Kokum," Monica said, kissing her grandma's head.

The intercom buzzed while Cheyenne said on the phone, "Get your butt over here, Chris. We have a guest and we made delicious food—"

"Yeah and we're not going to save any for you, Chris!" Monica interjected. "Justin, come on up," she said, answering the buzzing intercom.

Cheyenne brought more dishes to the table as Justin strolled in. "Hey everyone. Hey Miss Teacher," Justin said, taking a seat.

Well, at least it's not Mrs. Teacher. "Hey, young grasshopper."

"Yeah man, we're the Karate Kid."

"Are we going to wait for Chris or can we start eating already?" the youngest whined. Shelia pretty much shared the little one's sentiments.

"Chris said he's on his way. We can start while he gets here." Cheyenne explained, "Shelia, we customarily say a prayer, before we start."

"Of course," Shelia replied, respectful, despite her impartiality towards religion.

Once Cheyenne and Monica were seated, Shelia had a feeling of déjà vu. *Right. The meet-the-parents feeling. Well, hopefully I make a good impression,* she thought. *Or at least not a damning one.*

Monica's grandmother cleared her throat. "We thank the Creator, and the Earth, for graciously providing for us, and we thank the elk for its life, which will nourish us today. Amen."

"Amen," echoed back the table.

"Mom, I told Shelia you invited her here because you were suspicious of her," Monica said.

"You said what now?" Shaking her head, Cheyenne said to Shelia, "Don't worry, I'm not suspicious of you. I was just curious about the mysterious person who's teaching Monica all that complicated coding stuff. I just want to say, thank you for taking the time to do that. It's a special thing that you're doing here."

There we go with the flattery again. However, this time, Shelia allowed herself to feel good about it. "It's my pleasure, Monica and Justin really are great kids."

"You know, before Monica told me where she'd been disappearing off to, I assumed she got a new boyfriend she wasn't telling me about," Cheyenne laughed. "I much prefer her learning coding than messing with boys."
Shelia vaguely heard a door open and close in the background. "Chris, wash your face and come eat," Cheyenne called out.

"I'm taking a break from dating right now, anyway," Monica said. "It's nice to use the time to get to know myself, and find out what I'm about instead of obsessing over some dickhead."

"Wow, Monica, that's actually quite mature of you," Shelia said, dunking a piece of bannock in stew. Shelia recalled Miss Moon telling her to relish her time being single. Seeing Monica embody Miss Moon's counsel made Shelia appreciate its wisdom even more. *Even though when I was her age, I was too busy playing pokémon to be jaded by the dating world.*

"Very mature, Monica. Minus the term dickhead," Cheyenne noted.
Ambling into the dining room, Chris said, "She's not taking a break from boys, she's dating Justin now."
Justin and Monica erupted into protest at the same time.

"Me and Justin grew up together! Dating him would be, like… seriously weird."

"Yeah. Can't men and women just be friends without everyone thinking they're dating or something?"

Shelia was amused by their indignation. Admittedly, she'd wondered about those two, but she never sensed any romantic undertones between them.

"Who's this?" Chris asked, nodding towards Shelia.

Dialling down her annoyance that he didn't just ask her, she said, "Hi there, I'm Shelia. I'm teaching Monica and Justin how to make a video game."

"Nice," he nodded.

"We're doing it for Yoyo's," Justin said, solemnly.

"Yoyo is a real nice lady. She always gives me candy," the youngest commented.

Cheyenne looked over at Justin and Monica, impressed. "It's sweet of you guys to do that for Yoyo's. You two are very loyal."

"Thing is," Justin said, "It might not be enough… Yoyo's is closing in a month. At the pace we're going at, I dunno if we can make a video game in time…"

"Justin, Shelia is already giving you a lot of her time," Cheyenne admonished.

"I know, I know… and we appreciate it!" Justin said. "I'm just realistically speaking…"

Shelia mulled over what Justin was implying as she sipped her stew. She'd been thinking the same thing, but didn't want to pressure the kids. "I'm already committed to this project. I'm willing to do crunch-time for the game, if you guys are ready for that. It'll be a lot of long hours."

"Of course we are!" Monica exclaimed. "Bring it."

Justin didn't say anything. He sighed, getting up from the table, which garnered quizzical looks.

"Justin? What's wrong hun?" Cheyenne asked, as Justin made for the door.

He waved his hand and mumbled something unintelligible, before shutting the door behind him.

"Um... I can go after him," Shelia offered, getting up. Monica followed suit.

They found him sitting in the apartment hallway. Shelia approached him gently, taking a seat besides him.

"Hey Justin, what's up?" she asked.

"Yeah Justin, what's wrong?" Monica said, concerned.

Justin sighed, shaking his head. "What if it doesn't work? What if Yoyo's ends up closing, anyway? I don't know what to do if that happens... Yoyo's is home to me."

"Justin, I'm also scared, you know," Monica said. "That place is home for me, too."

Shelia exhaled, mulling over what to say. "I share your guys' feelings on this," she said. "There is no way to know if Yoyo's will survive or not, and that's scary. But even if the physical space doesn't survive..." she said, knocking on the wall, "I mean, we're still all here. Justin, it seems like you're always welcome at Monica's. And you're both always welcome at my place for an impromptu coding sesh. Or probably any of the other regulars that you've gotten to know. Of course, it wouldn't be the same—but the essence of Yoyo's doesn't need a bookstore… It plays itself out through us," Shelia said, realizing as she said it, that those were the words she needed to hear herself. "And look, it doesn't matter if the game does well or not. What matters is that you guys have fun and give it your best shot. We don't have to do it if it's too stressful," she said.

Justin waited a while before speaking. "No, I want to do it," he said. "I like doing what I can to help… even if we don't know what's going to happen in the end."

"And it's fun, too," Monica said.

Shelia nodded. "Okay," she said gamely.

They sat there for a bit, contemplative, before heading back to the dinner table.

When they returned, Cheyenne asked, "Everything alright?"

Justin nodded, softly replying, "Yeah."

"Mom, can I have more access to the computer since I'll be needing it to practice?" Monica asked.

"But I wanna play Acorn Planet," one of the younger siblings interjected.

"No," Chris said. "You're not the only one who needs to use the computer, Mon."

"Yeah, but at least I'm using it for more important things than Acorn Planet or watching porn," Monica retorted, making Chris turn red.

"O-kaaay, no talk of porn at the dinner table," Cheyenne declared.

"Like you'll actually use it for coding! You'll probably use it to watch dumb make-up videos or stalk your ex-boyfriends, plural!"

"Oh my god are you actually slut-shaming me right now? Like are you actually doing that?" Monica said, furious.

"Enough!" Cheyenne intervened. "Monica, there are other people who need to use the computer, too, for things that don't include adult videos. You'll just have to make do with your allotted time."

"But—"

"It's okay, Monica," Shelia said, putting a hand on her shoulder. "We'll just do most of the work on my computer like we always do, it's fine."

Monica nodded. "Okay."

Cheyenne heaved a sigh of relief. "Thank you so much, Shelia."

"Don't mention it."

She helped out with dishes, and bid the family farewell. "See you guys at the next lesson," she waved.

Shelia found herself with more of a schedule nowadays. She worked on freelance projects during the day—which just barely covered her monthly expenses, but it was an improvement—and coached Justin and Monica through their video game in her evenings.

It was nice to have her blob days done with. But now that they were done, she looked back on the period with a bit of romanticism. *I definitely could have enjoyed it more.*

Shelia mindlessly scrolled through her social media, snacking on tortilla chips. She'd been taking a ten-minute-turned-one-hour break from designing websites (*I blame the black hole of social media*) when she got a call.

From Rivercrest Retirement... Miss Moon?

"Hello?"

"Hello, this is Rivercrest Retirement Facility. A resident of ours is asking for a... Sheel-a?" the professional voice responded. "She's wondering if Shelia is dead."

You'd think it'd be the other way around. "This is her. Not dead and all."

"Great," the voice said passionlessly. "I'll transfer you over to Miss Moon."

After a few moments, Shelia heard a "Hello," from Miss Moon's characteristically shaky voice.

"Hey Moon." No response. "HEY, MOON."

"Ah, Shelia..." Miss Moon responded. "It is nice to hear from you... I was rather worried... I hadn't heard from you in a while..."

Shelia paused. She hadn't considered in all of her visits to Miss Moon, that she was creating a duty for herself—becoming someone that Miss Moon counted on.

"Right. Sorry about that, Moon. I got a little busy with clients and teaching coding... How have you been?"

"Oh, I've been the same as usual," Miss Moon said despondently, on cue. After a moment, she said, "Actually, no," changing the amount of despondency in her voice, "I had my visit with my friend Donna, and oh... it was so lovely... oh, and Jillian from my grocery days called back and she ended up visiting for tea too..."

"That sounds great, Moon," Shelia said, amused.

"It was great..." Miss Moon said, wistfully. "When will you be coming to visit, Shelia?"

She replied, "I'm not sure... I'll check my schedule and get back to you."

"Okay, dear. Goodbye."

Shelia had to reckon with the fact she was someone who "got back to people" now. *Obviously, it's not like I've never been busy in my life...* but it had been a while since she was a person that people sought out. She wasn't expecting that when it happened, it'd be senior citizens calling her up.

After two hours, when she'd finished designing one website, she got another call.

Mei? Shelia thought. *What does she want?* "What's up, Mei," Shelia answered.

"Shelia, I'm sorry about this but also kind of not sorry because you should have told them a long-ass time ago, but I accidentally told Ma and Ba that you're unemployed and now they're freaking out. I'm just warning you."

"Um," Shelia said, processing Mei's fast speech. "Well, I'm not technically unemployed now, I'm doing some freelancing…"

"Really," Mei said sarcastically, "That'll cheer them right up."

"Hey, it's legitimate work that I'm almost making a living off of."

Mei didn't say anything.

"Alright. Thanks for the warning, I guess. Bye."

"Bye."

The hang up beep was immediately replaced with the sound of an incoming call. Her parents.

"Hey," Shelia said cautiously.

"Shi-lei," her mother said, in an anxious tone, "You don't have a job anymore?!"

Shelia sighed. *Here goes.* "I didn't mean to not tell you guys… I was just scared of your reaction," she said sheepishly. She hated admitting her child-like behaviour.

"Shi-lei… are you alright? Do you need money?" her father jumped in.

"I…" she was expecting anger from them. Not sympathy. "Uh, no… I'm okay… thanks Ba."

"We didn't know that you were unhappy at your other job," her mom said.

"Well, I mean, it was just kind of stressful… But you don't have to worry. I have a couple of clients, so I'm staying afloat."

"I see," her dad said.

"Shi-lei, we only want you to be happy. Please let us know if you need anything."

"Thanks, Ma and Ba…" she said. A faint hint of tears tugged at her eyeballs. *God, when did I become such a cheeseball?* After she hung up, her thoughts wandered towards the future. She imagined her parents grayer, more wrinkled. *Will I even be able to provide for them?* she sighed. *Well, maybe Mei will be the one with her shit together, picking up my slack.*

Realizing that her back disliked being hunched over on the couch as she worked, she picked up her laptop and moved to her seldom-used desk in her bedroom. She pushed aside some papers, put on a website blocker, and continued working.

"So, the reunion went well?" Shelia confirmed, wheeling Miss Moon into the garden. She'd insisted on taking Moon outside. *'Cause her room is so damn depressing.*

It was a sterile garden; a bit too well-manicured, even for Shelia's tastes. But pleasant, nonetheless, in the way gardens are.

"Yes, it did go well… it was like no time had passed between Beatrice and I…" Miss Moon said. "Jillian, my old coworker, on the other hand…" she chuckled. "A mother of two, now! When we worked together, she was a little thing out of high school."

"Wow. Time, it goes," Shelia mused.

"You don't know the half of it," Miss Moon said knowingly. "It goes by faster... the older you get..."

Shelia continued navigating Miss Moon through the teenaged trees, the squeak of the wheels reverberating throughout the garden as they moved along.

Miss Moon asked, "Do you have many regrets, Shelia?"

Shelia thought about it. "Hmm... I don't think I've regret anything I've done, per se. Not to say that I'm particularly pleased with anything I've done. But I'm not, like, super displeased either... I'm neutral," she said.

"...I'm glad. You're far too young for regrets."

They wheeled along in silence, all the while, Shelia's mind pondering the subject.

"Actually," Shelia said, articulating the thought as it came, "maybe I regret never figuring out what I really want out of life. Only what I don't want—which is only helpful up to a point."

Miss Moon replied, "Same thing applies...And figuring out what you don't want...is so crucial."

Shelia waved to a person who passed her and Miss Moon, also wheeling along. "I suppose it's comforting to think that. At the same time, I can't deny that lost time is just... gone, forever."

"That time isn't gone... You were still living and learning in that time. Shelia, there's no such thing as bad decisions. Only decisions. The regret lies in how you deal with the aftermath of the decision. When you get to my age...the denouement of one's story…you've either failed or accomplished what you wanted to do, and then…it's more or less done with. You can look back on it with a bit of detachment, like something in the rear-view mirror."

Puzzled, Shelia asked, "Does this mean you don't have regrets, then?" *That would be counterintuitive, given how gloom and doom she is…*

Miss Moon nodded. "There's still much I would do differently…but none of them matter as much as my failure to…cultivate a proper social network."

Shelia absorbed what Miss Moon was saying. "I don't know, Moon. Is that really your fault? Your kids moved away, your married friends ditched you, you became unable to work…"

Miss Moon thought about it. "Perhaps it is, perhaps it isn't… But I wish I'd realized how important it was…I would have made friendships more of a priority. Now my only regular company is…people's whose job it is to take care of me," Moon said. She added, "And yourself, of course."

Shelia steered the wheelchair right, as the path forked. "But it's not enough, is it?" Shelia said.

"No, it's not…" Taking great effort to turn her head around, she smiled, saying, "But it is infinitely better than nothing." Shelia smiled back at her.

"…Who knows, maybe Beatrice and Jillian will come around more often."

"Good to be seein' you 'round here more often," Yoyo greeted, looking up from her book.

Shelia rolled her eyes, thinking, *Well, it's kind of your fault that I wasn't here all alo—ah, whatever, whatever, don't dwell…*

"Let's hope I get to come around here for a long time," Shelia tried to say as un-ominously as she could.

This was the first time that she felt nervous being at Yoyo's. *Media and colleagues watching my teaching performance…*

"So… how you feelin' about the big shot media covering your classes?" Yoyo asked.

Shelia shrugged. "We'll see how it goes, alright?" she said, a little agitated from her nerves. *I shouldn't be surprised that Yoyo isn't affected by being covered by national local media.*

"Shelia!" Monica called out from the back, momentarily jolting Shelia out of her head. "Let's do each other's make-up to get ready for the interview." Her and Justin popped out from the back, joining Shelia. They looked at each other's under-eye circles with a knowing nod.

They had stayed up the night before, finishing up 'Yoyo's the Game' and eating copious amounts of pizza, preparing the game for its launch today. She'd felt a lot of respect for the kids as they plugged away, working diligently. *When I was their age, did I give as much of a shit about… anything?*

"You want some concealer too, Justin? I probably have your shade."

"Sure," he shrugged, following them into the bookstore's bathroom.

"How are you guys feeling about the media coming soon?" Shelia asked, as Monica applied some light mascara on her. *Normally I wouldn't trust a kid with doing my makeup, but this is Monica we're talking about.*

"I dunno," Justin said. "But it's good that they are. It might help bring people to Yoyo's."

"Agreed," Monica said. "But it sucks that they're catching us when we look like shit," she frowned. "No offense."

"Aw, do we look like shit?" Shelia said, smirking.

"We stayed up so late. We totally do."

"Fine. We can mention it in the interview. The audience will eat up the story of such dedicated, loyal devotees of Yoyo's." Shelia appraised her face when Monica was done with it, noting she looked decidedly less sleep-deprived. They nodded at each other's visages approvingly, exiting the washroom. She jumped when the tiny bell tinkled then, which turned out to be no false alarm as it heralded the arrival of Olivia, Jeremiah, Elizabeth, and Amber and her camera crew.

"They're here," Justin said quietly. *No going back now.*

"You must be Shelia's entourage," Yoyo said, addressing the new arrivals. "She's in the back over there," Yoyo said, cocking her thumb. Shelia waved, to make the question of where she was clear to all involved.

"You must be Yoyo!" Amber said. "I've heard a lot about you. I'm really looking forward to the interview."

"Hopefully you've heard only the good things," Yoyo winked.

The group made their way to the back. "Hey guys, thank you for making it out," Shelia said, as they approached. "And for lending your resources and such…"

"For a worthy cause," Jeremiah said grandiosely, as he, Elizabeth, and Olivia brought out their laptops.

To Shelia, Amber said, "So I'm hoping to cover your teaching session, and then a demo of the game. And I'll sprinkle the individual interviews throughout."

"Sounds good."

"I'm excited to see you in action, Shelia," Olivia noted.

"Same," Amber said. "Otherwise I wouldn't be here with a camera crew," she laughed.

"'Action' is one way of putting it," Shelia said.

"Girl, don't be modest," Monica admonished. "What Shelia does is pretty bomb."

"Yeah, just admit that you're pretty bomb, Shelia," Olivia teased.

"I'm so bomb," she said sarcastically. But making fun of herself, and subsequently people making fun of her making fun of herself, took the edge off of having camera people in the room.

However, there was still an awkward silence between the medley of people, in which Shelia realized she should probably introduce everybody.

"Right. Everybody, this is Jeremiah, Elizabeth, Olivia, Amber, and Monica and Justin. These guys are my…friends/ former colleagues/a journalist, and Monica and Justin are my students, in a sense. If it weren't for them, there'd be no coding seshes in the first place."

"So, you're the one covering the coding class, and game launch for the Yoyo's fundraiser?" Monica asked Amber.

"Yes, I am," Amber confirmed. "Would you two be interested in being interviewed?"

"Um, hell yeah," Monica said, while Justin nodded.

"Great," Amber smiled, leading them and the camera crew into a quieter area.

Shelia watched them leave. Her eyes then darted between her current party, the door, and the clock. Six past five.

It suddenly occurred to her that all the people from last week's impromptu coding sesh might not show up. *How reliable are the RSVPs of random community members, anyway? I basically go to zero Facebook events I say I'm "going" to.*

"Wouldn't it be great if my own class stands me up the time the media shows up?" Shelia intoned.

"But Shelia," Elizabeth said, "your class didn't stand you up." Elizabeth nodded towards Justin and Monica. Shelia looked towards them, thinking, *Elizabeth is totally right.*

She overheard snippets of the kids' interview, "…Yeah, Yoyo helped me out when I was having a tough time at school…"

"And it's only five past," Jeremiah noted. "Not everybody can be as obscenely punctual as you, Shelia."

"Shelia," Olivia said, in her typical Olivia-fashion, "whether your other class members show up or not, just know that what you're doing here is amazing."

I don't know how I ended up with such a merry band of personal cheerleaders but… it's not half-bad. "Thanks, you guys."

But even with their encouragement, the fear of being on local national news sans homeless coding class lingered. And thus she continued looking back and forth between her former colleagues, the door, and the clock.

Colleagues, door, clock, colleagues, door, clock, colleagues… On her thirteenth glance-back towards the entrance, Joel appeared in lieu of a closed door.

"Hey there!" he waved enthusiastically. "Can't wait to learn more of that computer stuff."

Shelia waved him over silently in response, careful not to disturb the interview.

It turns out that she needn't have worried so much, as three out of the seven students from last week's class showed up by 6:12. *Shittier turn-out than last time…but now there'll be more quality instruction.*

"So, what are we learnin'?" Joel asked.

"So, what are we teaching?" Jeremiah echoed.

Shelia responded, "A review of basic HTML, like how to bold, italicize, make a colour font, all that. Then some coding theory. And hmm, maybe we can show you guys a demo of Pong to entice you for what's to come…"

"Pong is pretty enticing," Elizabeth said.

"Sounds like a time," another one of the students said.

Before they began, Shelia explained to the class why the media was there. Nobody objected to being interviewed: in fact, they were happy to help out the cause.

"Hey, if this interview is gonna help out Yoyo's, count me in," Joel said.

After Shelia's disclaimer, Jeremiah and Elizabeth fell into their teaching roles with ease. As a background in HR didn't translate well to teaching coding, Olivia was content to watch them do their thing.

"Yeah... there's a code for every colour you can think of. Look up 'HTML colour codes' to find the shade you're looking for," Shelia was explaining to a student named Ronda when Monica, Justin, Amber and her crew joined them at the back of the store again.

"These guys are naturals at interviews," Amber announced. "Shelia, you ready for us to cover your class?"

Are you ready for us to cover your class. Shelia registered what was being asked of her, but it took her a split second longer to connect it to the fact that whatever she did next was going to be on local news, broadcast to Ottawans everywhere. *I was so worried about whether these guys would show up that I forgot to be worried about the actual being on the news part.*

"Totally," Shelia said breezily (or at least, she hoped it came across as breezy.)

"Great," Amber said. She took out her mic while the camera crew got into position.

To Joel, who was currently being taught binary by Elizabeth, Amber asked, "How are you finding Coding 101?"

The camera zoomed in on Joel. "I'm not sure if the lady who started this, Shelia, even has a fancy name like 'Coding 101'... this class kinda just, happened. Boom. Y'know? But I'm finding it great. When you're focused on just surviving life, you don't get much opportunity to learn. But now I'm getting a chance to stretch my brain."

"Yeah, Shelia mentioned this impromptu class she had, and we just ended up signing on to the project. Today's our first class, and... so far, so good," Jeremiah said jovially.

"I just learned how to make a font purple," said Ronda. Eventually, Amber turned to Shelia. "As I understand it, this class 'just happened'... How so?"

Shelia glanced between the camera and Amber, before settling her eyes on Amber.

"Well. I guess I would have to start with Monica and Justin. They were regulars of Yoyo's, like I was. They knew I did code, so when they heard that Yoyo's was in trouble, they suggested that we make a computer game to save the place."

"I was coaching them through their game at Yoyo's, when some other regulars became curious about what was going on. We showed them a couple of concepts, and they asked me when the next coding sesh would be and... that's basically how it happened."

"And how did you yourself become a regular of Yoyo's?"

Shelia smiled to herself. "Ah... the day my old company announced lay-offs, I decided to get drunk. During my bar run, I saw that Yoyo's was open. The fact that a bookstore was open at 2 am intrigued my drunk self, and I went in. And... Yoyo doled out some of her wisdom to me," Shelia said, looking towards Yoyo, who smiled at her. "Yoyo's is an... oasis for the lost, lonely, or bored... Or just anyone, really. I think that's why so many people are passionate about saving Yoyo's from the forces of gentrification each time, because in some way or another, they've found themselves here."

Amber nodded thoughtfully. "I think this is a good time to show us that demo of 'Yoyo's the Game' you mentioned," she said, motioning for Monica and Justin to get into the camera's sightline, where Shelia was already sitting. Shelia pulled up the game on her laptop.

"So your character is Yoyo," Monica started, showing off the game version of Yoyo. "I designed her myself."

"Did a good job of it, if I do say so myself!" Yoyo called out. "She made me look real cute!"

Laughing, Justin demonstrated the gameplay. "The game is a normal 2-D platform game. You're navigating Yoyo as she jumps through hurdles, or jumps on monsters—"

"Each level is a little different, and harder than the last. If you make it through the six levels, at the end you can face—

"—The Gentra-Monster," Justin finished ominously.

Amber smiled. "Alright, then. Thanks for that demo. Anything else you want to add?"

"Yes. All the proceeds towards 'Yoyo's The Game' goes towards keeping Yoyo's open. Our fundraiser is happening on the twenty-second. We'll have bands playing, as well as food. So come out, have fun, support an essential cause," Shelia said.

"Alright, thank you, Shelia," Amber said. Amber turned towards the camera. "That was Justin Crowe, Monica Deerchild and Shelia Yang, members of the Yoyo's team working to save the community bookstore from being 'renovicted'."

So… I'm having coffee with Olivia. Interesting. The shock of being genuine friends with someone she was once frenemies with had not worn off.

I mean… are we friends? I guess it's more accurate to say that we are in the process of becoming friends. Who's to say if it will actually happen, Shelia thought, as she paid for a latte in a trendy café that was once the home of hipsters: nowadays frequented by young adult professionals.

She jumped when she felt a hand on her shoulder.

"Hey girl," Olivia grinned.

"Hi," Shelia said, giving a little wave.

"Seat by the window?" Olivia asked, before she ordered herself.

"On it."

Olivia joined Shelia a moment after she'd taken a seat, two drinks in hand. "Thanks," Shelia said, as Olivia handed Shelia her latte.

"I pick window seats because they're good for people watching," Olivia explained.

Shelia nodded. "I like people watching, too."

Olivia raised an eyebrow. "Really?"

"Mhm. I only realized this after I quit Cogville, when I started having enough free time to, you know, people-watch."

Olivia nodded; didn't say anything. Shelia didn't say anything. *Yeah… I can't get over how weird it is to be having a friend-date with Olivia.*

"This is weird, isn't it?" Olivia said.

Shelia laughed. "I mean, yes, but… maybe it's a good weird," she shrugged.

"Sure, we can go with 'good weird,'" Olivia chuckled.

In searching for something to say, the first thing Shelia came up with was "Hey, you remember that fish store you were raving about, way back?"

"Oh yeeeeeaaaaah," she said. "Hmmm, you never did go with me, did you?"

"I didn't," Shelia admitted, "but I did go myself eventually."

"And?" Olivia asked, stirring her coffee.

"It was as nice as you said it was," Shelia conceded. "Good for contemplation, you know."

"I'm glad you liked it," Olivia mused. "But come to think of it…" she said, "that fish place is pretty depressing, if you look at it from a kidnapped tropical fish's perspective."

"Hmm, like a dark alternate ending to that kid's fish movie," Shelia said. "Is the fish place ruined for us now, then?"

Olivia laughed, "I don't know!"
Shelia sipped her latte, smiling. At that moment, a flurry of people walked past on the street next to them, and the two newish friends stopped to observe.

"What do you like about people-watching?" Olivia asked, after the flurry subsided. "I like to imagine people's lives; how they're feeling… For example, that lady in the pink jacket—I bet she's reminiscing about her niece right now."
Shelia craned her neck to look at the lady in the pink jacket. From what Shelia could tell, she just looked like someone on their way somewhere. "*Reminiscing* about her *niece*?"

"Fine. Maybe I'm projecting," Olivia granted. "I reminisce about my niece all the time."

"I didn't know you had a niece."

"Yeah, I do," Olivia smiled. "She's the sweetest… being around her over the years definitely contributed to my… baby fever…" Olivia said, looking down at her coffee.
Ahhh… Sad Olivia. Shelia was still disconcerted at the appearance of Sad Olivia, a stark contrast to the colleague she was familiar with.

She tried to look as sympathetic as she could. Shelia did wish she could contort her face into genuine empathy, *but I just can't relate to the problem.*

But feeling that she was failing her concerned face, Shelia instead tried to take Olivia's mind off the subject. "Somehow, I'm not surprised that's why you like people-watching. It's very wild-child of you," she said. "As for me... I guess I like getting lost in the flow of people, not thinking about anything else."

"Ooh, be careful, I think you're wandering into hippie territory there yourself, Shelia," Olivia said.

"Ha," Shelia said. "I'm already there."

"Oh," Olivia said, raising an eyebrow. "How so?"

Shelia looked away, laughing nervously. "The me from even... a couple of months ago wouldn't believe that I'm admitting this, but I stopped hate-reading 'A Practical Guide to Life' and started reading it in earnest. Because it's been helpful. So... you were right about more than just the fish store."

"That's not even hippie territory, Shelia."

"What about all that mindfulness crap?"

"Hmm, okay, maybe," she conceded. With a soft smile Olivia said, "I wasn't right about everything." She gazed out the window thoughtfully. "After my miscarriage, and all this pregnancy bullshit... I understand why you didn't like me back then. Hell, I wouldn't be able to stand the old me if I met her, in my current state now. Maybe I was drawn to you because you weren't afraid to embrace your dark side."

It was true that Shelia'd found Olivia's posi-vibes farcical back then, but it was unsettling for Shelia to hear Olivia herself say that. "So you don't think I was too much of a sour-puss, then?" Shelia smirked.

"Well, maybe a little," she grinned, punctuating her words with a pinch gesture. "I mean, 'embracing the dark side' sounds like a bad thing, but it's necessary. Our culture puts positivity and feeling happy all the time on a pedestal… and that's so imbalanced. We need both to grow and heal."

Shelia nodded slowly. *I think I understand what she's getting at.* "Hmm, interesting. But don't you… you know, think you're being a little hard on your old self?"

Olivia blinked and then straight up started laughing at Shelia. Shelia looked back at Olivia blankly, not understanding why.

"It's just pretty funny that you're the one who's telling me to be easier on my old self."

"What?" Shelia said.

"C'mon, I can tell that you're not that easy on yourself, either." An idea slowly dawned on Olivia. "Shelia, did you read the 'Stop Being an Asshole to Yourself' chapter?"

"I did…"

"Did you do the writing-down-all-thoughts exercise?

"No. Who the hell can remember to write down every single thought they have?"

"You don't have to write down every single thought, Shelia. Just a thought here and there, and you'll get the gist of the exercise. But… I actually haven't done it myself," Olivia admitted. "Would you be willing to doing it with me, Shelia? We can hold each other accountable."

Shelia thought about it. Admittedly, the proposition held zero interest for her. But maybe a part of herself wanted to prove that she wasn't the old sourpuss she once was. Or maybe she wanted to provide an offering of goodwill to the new, budding friendship. *Hell, maybe I just want to cheer up Sad Olivia.*

Shelia sighed. "Alright, fine. I'm in."

In the morning, Shelia received a text from Olivia.

ready for all your thoughts?

Shelia wrote back, sure.

In truth, she'd totally forgotten that she was supposed to be writing all of her thoughts down. Begrudgingly, she got up, searched around her apartment for a stray notepad, and went back to her work station.

Usually I have about 50 tabs open, but that website blocker has really helped with my distraction levels. Shelia had found it necessary to install one after a boost in her number of clients, following a post she made offering her services. Shelia had felt weird promoting herself, but she (or rather, her slowly shrinking bank account) pushed herself to do it. *I guess Amber was right.* She'd found her new work flow reminiscent of the disciplined study schedule she'd followed for the majority of her life. *Go to school, go home, eat, study, extracurricular activity.*

How easy it had been to do away with half her lifetime of studious habits, once she was done with school. She'd been proud of her work ethic; it had gotten her far. *But it was stifling. I just didn't notice because I was so used to it.* This time, though, her return to a disciplined work routine was liberating.

Right, right, I'm supposed to be writing my thoughts down, Shelia remembered, while puzzling out how to configure a certain website plugin.

Fuck. Why can't I figure out how to fix this? And I'm the one who's supposed to be good at this shit, she wrote.

Impulsively she opened a social media tab, only to be met with the familiar website blocked message.

Well, I am in charge of creating the online event for the fundraiser. Maybe I should get that started instead of spinning my wheels on this project, she thought. In order to do so, she opened the site on her phone so she could bypass the website blocker.

'Hello new friends and long time patrons of Yoyo's,' she started typing.

'As you might have heard, Yoyo's Books is under threat of being closed down. For the third time.
The powers that be are hell bent on shutting down Yoyo's, because they just really want another coffee shop with a carefully curated aesthetic and pretty designs on the lattes, I guess?

Pretty designs on coffee are cool, but what Yoyo's stands for is more important. It's a place that will welcome you whether you're a burnt out young professional or someone who currently doesn't have a home. Whether you're bored with school or bored with life. Yoyo will give you some tough advice and make you some tea.

If you're a regular, you know the power of Yoyo's. If you're new to Yoyo's, you really ought to have the chance to experience it.

Donate to the campaign here, and come party with us on the 22nd for the fundraiser! Admission by donation. '

Shelia finished writing up the description, feeling satisfied. When she started sending out invites to her online 'friends', though, her satisfaction turned to disappointment. *Damn, I forgot that I have like, no friends,* she thought.
Wait. I'm supposed to be writing this shit down.

I forgot that I have no friends.

She looked at the invite list again. *This isn't going to reach the amount of people that it needs to,* she thought, frowning. *But I suppose the social heavy-hitters can send it widely, picking up my slack.*

Hi Olivia, **she texted.** Can you invite your impressive network of people to the event I just sent you?

sure thing! **she responded.**

Once she sent the invites, she started scrolling through her feed. One RSVP. Two RSVPs. Four.
Not bad, not bad, she thought, checking back with every notification.
It was an hour later, when she found herself in the midst of a '10 Shocking Secrets of Celebs' article, when she realized her folly.
Godamnit, I wasted so much time!
I wasted so much time, she wrote while thinking, *Man, this exercise is weird.*
Eventually, after much frustration, she figured out what the bug was (an unintentional infinite loop). The rest of her projects went smoothly from there.

Visit Miss Moon, her phone beeped, reminding her after a couple of hours of being lost in a coding flow. She'd put the reminder in when she realized she hadn't visited Miss Moon

in the craze of the video game launch and Yoyo's Books
fundraising.

I hope she's not pissed at me for not visiting, Shelia wrote before
heading out.

8

When she arrived at Riverview Retirement, she found room
408 conspicuously empty.

Fuck. She's dead. What the fuck.

Trying not to blurt out, *"Is she dead?!"*, Shelia asked the
receptionist for Miss Moon's whereabouts.

"She had a stroke. She's at Mayfair Hospital right now," the
receptionist said sympathetically.

"Oh... I see."

"You're the girl who visits her occasionally, right? We tried
to find your contact, but no luck."

Shelia thanked the receptionist anyways and made her way to
the hospital.

Damn, why is parking so expensive? she thought, as she pulled
into an open lot. *People are already stressed about dying people, for
Christ's sake.*

"Is there a Miss... I mean, is there a Darlene Moon here?
Am I able to visit?" she said, once inside.

The nurse nodded. "Room 212 B".

Shelia power walked to said room. The door was half open, and she spotted Miss Moon lying on the hospital bed, eyes closed.

Her visage seemed more etched with lines than usual. Shelia tip toed in, trying not to cause a disturbance, but Miss Moon slowly opened her eyes anyway. As if it were a Herculean task.

"Shelia?" Miss Moon said groggily. "I was wondering... when you'd show up."

"I hope you weren't waiting too long."

"Well...you sure did...take your time."

"Ah, sorry, Moon," Shelia said, taking a seat next to her. "Uh... how are you?" Shelia asked the customary question, feeling weird about it.

"Bad."

Shelia nodded. *Figures.* "...Want me to read to you?"

Miss Moon nodded, lethargically.

" '*Munsch, with his perpetually glum temperament, was ill-suited for the task. This, they all agreed on. So they conspired to...*' "

Shelia started reading, from where she left off.

Well into reading the scene, Shelia glanced over to find Miss Moon's eyes shimmering.

Shelia glanced back at the book to confirm it wasn't just a particularly sad scene she was reading.

"Oh, Miss Moon, what's wrong?" Shelia asked, alarmed.

Miss Moon looked at Shelia, so sorrowful that it made her uncomfortable.

"I'm not ready to die," she said, shaking her head. "I... thought I was. Ready for all this to be done with, and go in peace. But there's just so much…"

"So much what?"

She shook her head again.

Shelia frowned. "I don't think anybody is ever ready to die… except maybe just before it happens," she tried. "But how are you so sure you're going to die? You just survived a heart attack."

"When you know you're going to die, you just know."

Shelia didn't know how to respond to that.

She sighed. "Okay. What now, then?"

Miss Moon looked at her, indicating that she did not know.

"Okay."

They both listened to the hum of the hospital machines. The occasional scurry of a nurse. Distant chatter.

This soundscape abruptly gave way to a cacophony of determined footsteps, growing louder as they approached their destination. "It's this one," Shelia heard a voice say before the people behind the footsteps entered the room.

"Mom?" the woman leading the charge asked breathlessly. She had the same eyes as Miss Moon.

Shelia immediately got up from her seat and stood aside, awkwardly.

"Ohhhh, hello, Candace," Miss Moon said. "And dear Katie and Evan are here…William…you've made it as well…

And hello Peter," Miss Moon greeted each person as they leaned over and gave her a makeshift hug.

Shelia wondered if she should stealthily leave at this point. But in her spot she remained, observing the scene.

"We booked the first flight here. Mom, how are you?"

"Bad."

Eventually, Candace turned around and acknowledged Shelia. "You must be Shelia," she said.

Shelia was surprised that Candace knew who she was. "My mom's mentioned you a lot," Candace explained.

"Oh," Shelia said. "Well... It's nice to meet you. I was curious about the person behind the letter."

Candace gave a pained smile in response, and turned back towards her mother.

"I'll leave you guys," Shelia said, softly making her exit.

Shelia sat in her car, still in the hospital parking lot, deliberating over whether she should still go to the bar with Jeremiah and the gang. *I'm not sure if I'm feeling up to it,* she wrote. But she didn't want to flake on the new group, and with it, her fledgling social skills.

"Heyyyyyyyy Shelia," Jeremiah greeted heartily. He had to shout over the din of the bar, a new craft beer place. Elizabeth gave her a hug, the others; friendly waves.

While pulling up her seat, she dropped her thought notepad. She couldn't help but blush when Jeremiah picked it up.

"Oooh, what's this?" Jeremiah said, quickly turning it over before handing it back to Shelia.

Caught off-guard, Shelia couldn't concoct a story, so she was stuck with the truth. "It's a... thought logbook," she said.

"Like a journal?" Vince asked, confused.

"No, like, when I have a thought, I just write it down. It's impossible to write every thought down, but it's just to get a general idea of the contents of my head."

"Like mindfulness training?" Elizabeth asked.

"Hmm... I'm not sure. Olivia kind of enlisted me."

"I would be afraid to examine the contents of my own head. You're a brave woman," Dipon noted.

"You should be afraid, who knows what darkness is hiding in that noggin," Vince said, punching Dipon's shoulder.

"My head is saintly compared to your very disturbing mind."

"So," Jeremiah said curiously, ignoring the mock-fight that ensued. "What have you learned from the logbook, Shelia?"

Shelia's face went a little hot at the question. She was prepared for a little casual conversation, not an examination of her thoughts.

"Well... There's a trend of a lot of the thoughts being negative. Big surprise."

"I'm sure we'd find the same thing, too," Elizabeth offered kindly.

"Seriously, Shelia, it's no small thing that you're doing. Learning to divorce myself from my thoughts was really helpful in getting out of my depression," said Jeremiah.

"I didn't know that you'd had depression," Shelia said, inquisitive.

"Mhm," he confirmed.

"Me too," Elizabeth nodded. Vince, as well.
Shelia immediately felt closer to the group after their admissions', and relief that she wasn't the only one exposing herself.

"Before this turns into a group therapy sesh... another round, shall we?" Jeremiah asked, with the group agreeing heartily.
Drinks in hand, they moved on to non-therapy related subjects. Dipon turned away from the group discussion, towards Shelia. "Hey, Shelia. I actually wanted to talk to you about your Yoyo's game," he said. "Can we chat somewhere where we can hear each other properly?"

"Sure," she said, walking over to a quieter corner, interest piqued.
She wondered idly if she should still be wary of Dipon, given the events of their first meeting, but her brain overturned that motion. *I'm over it.*

"Brad's friend works in the game industry, and his company, Modern Fable Games, heard about your PC game. They want to buy it, Shelia," Dipon said, cutting to the chase.

"Oh," she said, absorbing the news. "Wow."

"They've been facing some controversy over their sexist games. So they want to change their image as a site for wanking preteen trolls into something a little… classier. So they're reaching out to female game creators."

"Won't they offend their core base?" Shelia said wryly.

"Probably," Dipon said. "Maybe they should be offended. They could stand to gain some new fans."

Dipon continued, "The reason I know all of this dirt is because I gave them your number and they told me their situation. You should expect a call from them soon," he said suavely.

"Dipon… thank you, for doing that," she said, not understanding why Dipon wanted to help her.

"I didn't do anything," he said. "I was just a link in the network," he winked.

…The game might actually raise some money for Yoyo's. Holy shit.

"I have a total of FOUR thoughts about how fat I'm feeling," Olivia said, upon review of her thought logbook.

"I have a couple, too," Shelia said sheepishly.

Shaking her head, Olivia said, "What is it with our total brainwashing? We have completely normal bodies."

"I dunno," Shelia said, taking a bite out of her cake that she was eating at yet another cute café.

She looked over her thoughts again, in awe of the sheer volume of nonsense. "I'm embarrassed about my thoughts."

"Please," Olivia said, "we all have bullshit swirling around in our head. It's not who we truly are."

She considered for a moment trolling Olivia about 'who we truly are', but Shelia was trying to tame her abrasive impulses towards Olivia. Besides—she liked the idea that she wasn't the sum of her (negative) thoughts.

Fiddling around with the pages of the logbook, she said, "Olivia, I understand the lesson you're beating me over the head with. My thoughts are not that kind to myself. But I can't help it, they just… come up. I'm not sure what I'm supposed to do about that."

In a tone that conveyed, much to her dismay, that she didn't know either, Olivia replied, "Well, that's the million dollar question, isn't it?" She took a long sip of her drink, licking the foam off her lips. "I used to think I had the self-love thing down pat. But recent circumstances have made it difficult."

"Well, at least you had it once," Shelia pointed out, trying not to sound wistful. She feared that her reassurance didn't sound genuine because—frankly, she was a little jealous. That Olivia even had the ability to self-love, while Shelia could hardly conceptualize it. *'A Practical Guide to Life' helps a bit with understanding self-relationship stuff, but still…*

"Shelia, I'm afraid to say this because you'll roll your eyes at me," Olivia started, "but something that got me there was doing affirmations. I mean… I haven't been in the mood to do them lately," she disclaimed, "but they were helpful when I actually did them. I mean, these negative thoughts are coming up subconsciously, right? And all affirmations do is reprogram those subconscious beliefs. I think you should consider trying them."

Well, Olivia wasn't wrong in that I'd normally roll my eyes. In lieu of that, though, she looked squarely at Olivia.

"Olivia, you've already roped me into this," Shelia said, waving around her thought logbook. "So… maybe it's not too much of a stretch to consider… affirmations."

"Great. If you do them, I will do them with you," she said, resolute; her eyes cheerfully meeting Shelia's.

Auction Items
- *Books (Yoyo's Picks)*
- *Tea Sets*
- *Board Games*

She put down her pen at the ring of her signature nondescript ringtone. *Monica, huh?* she thought, checking the ID.

"Hey Monica, what's up?" Shelia said.

"I talked to Sally's Teas, and they said they would be willing to donate a set!"

"That's awesome. Thanks for doing that, Mon."

Shelia, at Monica's age, would have only procured fundraising auction items if it served to enhance her curriculum vitae. In fact, Shelia's whole organizing of the fundraiser made her recall her days of extensive extracurricular activities: leading clubs, student councils, etc., because that's how high achievers were supposed to spend their time. In university, she did away with most extracurriculars *because pretty much only med kids needed to do that.*

Now she quite enjoyed organizing something that she actually gave a shit about.

Hi, this is Tad from the band. Was wondering if we could do a practice set-up to check levels?, **her phone beeped.**

yeah, sure, can you guys come this Thursday?

The time her phone reflected back at her made her panic. *Shit, I have to get going!* She smoothed over her pencil skirt and ran out the door, keys jangling.

"Why do you want to work here?" a suited man with salt-and-pepper hair asked Shelia. A big desk divided her and the interviewer, and the window behind him displayed scenes of the downtown.

Because I need to put food on the table? Shelia knew the interview drill, however, and so she knew this question was a chance to prove she had A) actually researched the company and B) wasn't just looking for a job, any job (which she was, of course).

"The work that Press Pros puts out is known for it's originality and quality, so I know I can be proud of any project I undertake here. And, Press Pros is known for its sustainable company work culture, which is an anomaly in the tech sector."

Approval of her given answer peeked out from behind the interviewer's poker face. He continued, "What about your last job did you least enjoy?"

Talk about something that won't apply to the job you're applying for.

"I disliked not always being able to be innovative in the work I produced. My old company had their systems, which they had for a reason, but I do think it might have been beneficial to be open to other ways of achieving the same task."

He nodded thoughtfully. "And the last question—what do you think are your weaknesses?"

Instead of the old weakness-that's-actually-a-strength, just say an actual weakness, but how you'll improve upon it.

"I'm a bit of a lone wolf. It isn't bad in and of itself, but it's not typically how a workplace, well, works. Lately I have been learning the importance of teams, and community, as a whole," she said.

The interviewer looked at her curiously—or scrutinizingly—Shelia couldn't tell.

"Well, that's all I have for you. Do you have any questions for us?"

Never not have any questions for them. It makes you look un-proactive.

"Yes. I was wondering what kinds of goals Press Pros had moving forward?"

"Part of the reason we're looking for new team members is our expansion efforts, focusing on the increased demand for plugins in addition to website designs. Our target moving forward is to become a go-to for both."

"Ah, I see," Shelia nodded, looking like she cared about the nuances of company objectives more than she actually did.

"Alright then, Shelia—thank you for your time."

"Thank you for considering me," she responded with an appropriate smile.

After this exchange something seemed to shift in him, a relief that he could drop his interviewer persona and say, "By the way, we took the liberty of looking you up, and found your Yoyo's Books interview. It seems like you're very passionate about coding, and giving back, Shelia," he said, giving her his first genuine smile.

affirmation, Shelia's phone beeped, reminding her of the challenge she promised to do with Olivia.

Ugh. Just the thought of doing affirmations made Shelia cringe. But as much as she would rather skip them, she did not want to have to report back to Olivia that she did so.

Okay, so I need to say these to myself while looking at a mirror, Shelia thought, resigned to her fate of affirmations.

She positioned herself in her bathroom. Her reflection looked back at her, skeptical.

"I love myself," she said aloud, strained. "I'm perfect just the way I am."

She waited for a bit, but the feeling of embodying attuned vibrations never came up.
She idly studied her grimace.

i can't do the affirmations, **she texted Olivia.** they feel too disingenuous.
and extremely cheesy.

Olivia texted back immediately, it's okay, Shelia. why not come up with one that doesn't feel disingenuous?

Ok, she responded, thinking about what wouldn't feel disingenuous. More easily than she expected, a fitting affirmation came to her.
She took a breath. "I like myself. I'm a decent human being. I am carving a life out for myself."

   "After all of this time... I'm still confused," Shelia said, leaning on the bookstore counter.
   "About life, I'm presumin'?"
Rolling her eyes, she said, "Always."
   "Well, kid, the wise are the ones who know they don't know shit... as they say."
Shelia smiled, humoured at Yoyo's spin on the saying. "Yes, but... after you think you know, and then you realize that you don't, you'd have to eventually know after that, right?"

Yoyo laughed. "Listen, d'you you feel closer from when you started this mess? If you can say yes, then you're good, kid. Continue following those clues, and you'll get there. But also, there doesn't exist," Yoyo said, clapping her on the shoulder.

"Um…" Shelia said, while Yoyo looked massively amused at her confusion. "I suppose it'll make sense eventually," she smirked. She pulled out her *Yoyo's Fundraiser List,* as Yoyo went around and smudged the store.

"Okay, we have all of the auction items… all the food in place… Jamie, is the bands' sound check good?" Shelia said, walking over to where the bands would be playing.

"Checking that now," Jamie the sound guy said, giving a nod.

She fixed up the placement of the food, while she wondered what else she should worry about.

"Oh my god," Monica laughed, snapping a photo of Shelia.

"Why did you just snap a pic of me?" Shelia said, jolted out of her planning mode.

Monica quickly typed something before handing her phone to Shelia.

It was a picture of Shelia captioned, 'Shelia #motherhenning. So excited for the #YoyosFundraiser! We got all da food and music. All u losers betta come out'.

"Aw Monica, lay off, it's good that Shelia's a mother hen, " Justin said.

Dryly, Shelia said, "Are you sure people will come out if you call them a loser?"

"Don't worry, it's ironic."

"Ooooo girl, you're as tense as a sphincter." Finished smudging the space, Yoyo came up and put a hand on Shelia's shoulder. "Look, kid. You've done everything you can, 'an I'm grateful for all yer efforts. This is a fundraiser— but we're also celebratin' all a' ya who make this place what it is. So I want you to enjoy yourselves, alright?"

"Alright, alright," Shelia said, raising up her hands, willing herself to relax; let things go at this point.

Yoyo ushered everyone into a circle. They held hands as Yoyo quietly said a prayer. Yoyo then made her way around, offering each person smoke from a smouldering bundle of sage. Shelia followed everyone's lead, scooping up the smoke and placing it on her head and heart.

"Guys, group photo!" Monica announced once the ceremony was complete, passing Shelia her phone. "Shelia, you've got the longest arms."

Monica, Shelia, Justin, and Yoyo all huddled together. Attempting not to look awkward and maybe even semi-attractive, Shelia snapped the photo—capturing their collective nerves and excitement.

It was her cue to go on the makeshift stage. She might normally have been anxious, but her would-be nerves got absorbed into her buzz about—well, everything.

She got up and adjusted the mic. "Hello everyone," the mic amplified into the crowd. Literally all of her people were there. The gang: Elizabeth, Dipon, Vince, Jeremiah, Olivia. The Yoyo's regulars. *And my family.* Shelia was still getting used to all of them there in the same space at the same moment in time.

"Well. Thank you all for being here. Whatever your reason is. It might be your first time here, or your hundredth, or whatever. It's funny how this place has pulled us all here together anyway," she started.

"This bookstore. It's so unassuming, isn't it?" she asked. "Well, maybe it is a little assuming. I don't know any bookstore with a death-and-taxes rubber chicken. Or that's open at 2 am."

Chuckles rippled through the crowd, bolstering Shelia further.

"Still, none of those things could hint at the power of Yoyo's. Although we do have a great selection of books—it's much more than that. How Yoyo's pulls you in. How it finds all who need it. There's a… secret rebel spirit here. That's why they keep wanting to shut it down," Shelia joked, garnering smiles from the crowd.

"Some of you know that we've started doing coding sessions, hosted by yours truly, and some friends," she said coyly. "You may or may not have seen *on the news*, but me and my first students, Monica and Justin, have recently launched 'Yoyo's the Game'. Come on up here, guys," she smiled, as they scampered onto the stage.

"I'm happy to announce, that we've raised… THREE
THOUSAND NINE HUNDRED AND THIRTY-FIVE
DOLLARS from our game launch!"

At this, the crowd exploded in applause and cheers, and it
didn't die down for a while.

Shelia, Monica, and Justin looked at each other, grinning.
As the kids left the stage, Shelia continued, "Should Yoyo's
survive this latest setback—" she said, the crowd cheering,
"—you'll be seeing more features in the upcoming months.
Along with the coding seshes, we'll be hosting more shows
like 'Haus Elves', who will be playing right after this, as well
as other events, coordinated by our new recruit Olivia
Ghezielle," Shelia smiled, pointing out Olivia in the crowd,
amongst the cheers.

"To create a more sustainable business model, we're
introducing a monthly subscription to those who want to
support Yoyo's. Subscribers get discounts on books, events,
and most importantly, the satisfaction of supporting vital
community spaces."

"Thank you all again for being here. Now I'm gonna pass it
off to the woman of the bookstore herself." Amidst booming
applause, Yoyo got up and received the mic from Shelia, eyes
crinkling. "Thank you," she whispered to her, before speaking
into the mic.

"I think Shelia's done most of the babbling for me, so I'm
gonna keep this short an' sweet. By the way—she's the one
who convinced me to do this fundraiser, so let's give it up for

Shelia, eh?" Crowd obliging heartily, Yoyo continued, "I gave this place birth, but Yoyo's is really about all of you. To the newcomers—welcome. We hope to see ya around here more often. To my regulars, you know who you all are. You made this place what it is. I get as much out of this as you all do. Thank you for always supporting this co-creation o' ours. Thank you for coming out today. This place is a dream come true," she said, eyes teary. "I couldn't do it without all of you."

Leaving behind thunderous applause in her wake, Yoyo passed the mic back off to Shelia.

"Alright guys… let's give it up for our first act, Haus Elves!"

"How did you pull this one off, Sheel?" Mei asked, dubious, once the audience calmed down, and the first band went up.

"Well, I didn't pull it off myself. It was really everybody. For example, Olivia connected us to the bands that are playing today," Shelia said, gesturing to Olivia.

"Not surprised that cool bands are among the people that Olivia knows," Elizabeth said, overhearing the conversation.

"Seriously Olivia, how do you know everybody?" Jeremiah asked.

"Talk to people, keep in touch, classic boring networking stuff," Olivia answered prudently. "Sometimes it's boring or awkward, but sometimes you'll form a genuine connection."

"So, a numbers game…" Shelia said.

"Something even antisocial computer nerds can get behind," Dipon noted.

"It's true," Shelia said.

"That's what I don't get," Mei told Shelia. "Organizing something like this is so unlike the computer nerd I know as my sister. It's so… cool."

Olivia laughed, nudging Shelia. "I can get how it can be hard to see our own family as cool."

With a wry smile, Shelia responded, "Well sister, contrary to what you might think, I have many layers to my personality." Shelia understood where Mei was coming from, though. She herself could have never imagined herself here, right now.

"Shelia, we saw you on the news. We are very proud of you," her father interjected, beaming.

"We didn't know you were doing these kinds of things. Why don't you tell us?!?" her mother chided.

Shelia laughed. "Sorry, Ma. I guess I didn't realize this kind of thing was happening to me. It just kind of happened." She gave each of her family members a hug, saying, "Thank you guys for driving all the way out here for this."

"Of course we would," Mei replied, as she pulled back. Shelia left her people to enjoy the jazz-rock-house beats of Haus Elves, while she grabbed some appies from the food spread. *We did a good job on the spread,* she thought idly, taking a cake slice.

"So you're Yoyo's student du jour?" a man asked beside her, startling Shelia.

"What?" she said, mid-chew.

The man smiled. "Name's Aaron Odjick. You know what you said about how Yoyo's pulls you in? I felt that. I'd totally felt that. You're just kind of walking along, and before you know it, you're inside here, staring that chicken in the face," he said. "Yoyo had also taken me personally under her wing at a transitional moment in my life," he explained. "There's a lot of us Yoyo's alumni here, actually."

Shelia laughed, shaking her head. *Of course. Of course Yoyo's done the sensei-thing multiple times with multiple different people throughout the years.*

"How do you know that I'm in a transitional moment in my life?" she said.

"You seem like a woman who's been on a journey," he said, eyes sparkling.

He's charming, Shelia thought, taken off-guard. "I—I guess you can say that," she smiled.

She wandered over to the crowd again, while the second act was setting up. On her way, Dipon caught her. "Hey, Shelia," he said. "What did the kids think of Modern Fable Games' proposal?

Shelia started to respond, but stopped when she spotted Monica, Justin, and their friends passing by.

"Guys," she said, halting them. "This is Dipon, he's the one who connected us to Modern Fable Games. Wanna fill him in on what we decided?"

"Hello Dipon, thank you for that pivotal connection," Justin said formally.

"Glad I could be of help, bud. How did the meeting go?"

"Well," Monica said, "the company was offering mad stacks for the game, which was always the goal. But…"

"Did we *really* want the home of Yoyo's the Game to be a notorious site for trolls? Even if it did have some pretty sweet games…"

"We said that their new, non-troll image was still too new for us to be cool with Yoyo's being there. But, we'd like to have any future games be on their site. There's gonna be way more 'cause of Shelia's legit coding army."

"We didn't sell out, man. And we still raised a lot of money from our independent launch! Especially after the interview with Amber aired," Justin finished triumphantly.

One of Monica and Justin's friends noted, "Man, you guys are ballers."

"Agreed," Dipon said.

Shelia looked over the teens as a proud mother hen would, as they shuffled along.

The sounds of the next band setting up gave way to clean, precise beats of electro-pop. A hip duo that Shelia didn't remember the name of. (She'd never actively listened to such music—but she was into it.) At one particularly catchy junction, Monica grabbed Shelia's hand and started dancing. Shelia, normally hard-pressed to dance sober, could not refuse.

Their dancing duo infected the people surrounding them with similar danciness. She became merely a point in an undulating dance mob, young and old; past and present.

She looked at her smiling family, at the cheering regulars, at the bobbing faces of her—friends, she was confident saying now—and caught herself not searching. And she realized that she hadn't been for a while.

She watched a radiant, swaying Yoyo, thinking, *Damn, I hope I can dance half as good when I'm her age.*

9

"Hey Moon, hi Candace," Shelia said, gingerly taking a seat next to her hospital bed.

"Hi Shelia, thanks for coming," Candace said. Her under eye circles were gaunt, illuminated by the fluorescent lights.

"Of course," Shelia said. "How bad are you feeling?" Shelia asked Moon, in lieu of *How are you?*

"Pretty bad," Miss Moon chirped, happy that a question, for once, indulged her sadness. "My breathing's got more… difficult…and the food here is…worse than at the home…can you believe it…"

Miss Moon's breathing was indeed more haggard than before. "Um, what happened to your breathing?" Shelia asked, frowning.

"Complications during the surgery," Candace answered for her mother, tiredly.

"Oh," Shelia said. She wondered when was the last time Candace took a nap. "Candace, is your brother coming to visit?"

Her face nominally perked up. "He's coming in from Calgary tomorrow… It'll be nice to have some help looking after Mom."

Shelia nodded. A thought just occurred to her. "You know, if you wanted to take a break, take a nap or something, I can stay for a couple of hours."

"Oh," Candace said, caught off-guard. "That's nice of you to offer, but it's okay, really."

Oh my god this polite bullshit. Will it really kill you to take a nap? Shelia didn't know how maneuver around the niceties.

Luckily Miss Moon intervened and said, "Oh, Candace, stop… you look terrible…"

"Gee, thanks, Mom!" Candace snapped. "I'm only trying to keep you from dying and all."

Miss Moon said casually, "Maybe you should…just let me die…"

Candace looked strained. She rubbed her forehead and said, "You know what, I will take a nap. Thanks Shelia," she said, walking out.

Shelia was not sure what to make of being witness to another family's uncomfortableness. *Should I have a moment of silence for the discomfort or…?*

While she wondered what to do, Miss Moon said, "I actually…don't want to die…"

"Oh, why'd you tell your daughter to let you die, then?"
Shelia said, slightly annoyed.

Miss Moon was annoyed right back. "I don't want…to be a…
burden, Shelia! You have no idea…what it's like…" she said,
blinking back angry tears, "no idea…"

Fuck, I just made an old lady cry. She sighed. "Look, assuming
you weren't an abusive, shitty parent, you did your part in
raising your kids, and now they can take care of you. There's
no shame in that, Moon."

Miss Moon sighed too, except it was perhaps the longest sigh
Shelia had ever witnessed, let alone from someone who had
trouble breathing.

  "I don't want to die, Shelia."

Miss Moon's eyes reflected those of a frightened, caged
animal. Shelia had to look away. To be in the throes of death
—no, Shelia did not know what that was like. If she had to
imagine what one would feel in old age, she'd imagine a calm
acceptance would eventually emerge. Not terror.

She didn't know what to say. She walked up and lightly held
Miss Moon's hand. Perhaps Miss Moon was nominally
comforted by the gesture—Shelia couldn't tell.

  "I'm…tired," she said finally, closing her eyes. In not an
unkind tone she said, "Go away, please."

  "You know Moon, I would like to respect your wishes, but I
can't leave," Shelia said gently, removing her hand. "Take a
nap if you want, but for god's sake, don't bop off in your
sleep. Candace'll feel super guilty."

"Fine," Miss Moon intoned, eyes still closed.

Eventually Shelia heard the haggard snoring. *If she actually dies in her sleep, I'm going to feel very guilty.*

She studied Miss Moon. Even while slumbering, Shelia thought she looked rather discontent.

She idly scrolled through her phone. *15 dead in a train crash... random old classmate's baby announcement... nice travel pics... Ugh, why am I doing this?* she abruptly stopped scrolling. She realized her eyebrows had been furrowed. She un-furrowed them and took out the book she'd been reading aloud to Miss Moon over her visits.

She was twenty pages from finishing the book when Candace walked in. Shelia looked up, noting Candace seemed decidedly less exhausted than before.

"Thanks, Shelia, for your help," Candace said, indicating that Shelia was now relieved of her duties.

She looked back and forth between Miss Moon and Candace uncertainly, before getting up.

"Of course," Shelia nodded.

"I really appreciate it," Candace said earnestly.

Shelia smiled. "Well, I mean, I consider Moon a friend. If a slightly eccentric one."

Candace nodded, smiled back.

Shelia started to turn away, but stopped. "Uh," she laughed. "I was kind of curious... how did that letter of yours end up in 'A Practical Guide to Life', anyway?

Candace looked surprised at the question, but obliged it. "I remember I was reading that book when I visited here a couple of years ago. I found that letter lying around in Mom's room. Mom never did respond to it," Candace said, with a resigned smile. "I ended up using that letter as a bookmark. And *then* I ended up getting annoyed with the book, and donating it to the first place I found," she said sheepishly.

"I spent most of my time reading that book being annoyed at it, too," Shelia smiled.

Candace laughed. "Glad to know I'm not the only one."

"It was pretty cool to find the letter in there, actually," Shelia said. "All mysterious and everything."

"Oh, yeah?" Candace said. "Well, I'm glad some good came of it. I'd tried the letter-writing as a... I thought it would be a way to be connected. It was an experiment that didn't work," Candace said, sighing. "I guess it figures that a little letter here and there wouldn't patch up years of... you know."

"Sure," Shelia said. She murmured, "At least you tried, Candace."

Candace smiled briefly, at this. "I guess I have to find a way to be at peace with the way things are between my mom and I, even if it's not ideal. Find acceptance."

Shelia nodded. "I really hope you do find that."

"Thanks, Shelia," Candace said quietly.

They parted ways.

Miss Moon, it turns out, would not bop off in her sleep.

Shelia learned of this fact seven hours after the event.

She was in the midst of a coding problem when she received a call from Candace.

There is only one reason Candace would call me, Shelia thought, her stomach dropping.

"Hey, Candace…" Shelia said, sympathy already in her voice.

"You can guess what happened," Candace said. She paused, and then elaborated, "She died of cardiac arrest."

Shelia stopped breathing for a moment, despite having guessed the news. Finally, she said, "I'm… so sorry, Candace."

"I'm sorry, too. I know… you were a good friend to her in those last days," Candace said, her exhaustion coming through the phone.

They exchanged details for the memorial. Well after they'd hung up, Shelia held the phone aloft as if she were still on speaker.

Slowly she put her phone back on the table, and stared blankly at the computer screen.

Okay. Okay. She's dead. She's old and she was in the hospital. So… what do you expect, right? She herself even expected to die. So…

The cursor at the forefront of paragraphs of code seemed to blink at her expectantly.

She shut her laptop, walked over to her couch, and put on *Vengeful Mamas.*

The one nice thing about not having friends was not having to deal with messages. Now, comparatively, Shelia's phone was blowing up.

hey girrrrrrrrrl! why haven't u been at Yoyos?! we wanna break the good news 2 u in person!!!!!

Monica's message was from a couple of days ago. Other messages included:

yo Mrs. Teacher, when is the next coding class??
P.S YOYO'S MADE IT

Hey Shelia, congrats on the fundraiser! We'll celebrate over the usual Monday drinks ;)

Shelia, congratulations on the fundraiser! I knew it would be successful. Yoyo's has such an energy to it that people will stick by it, no matter what.

It was a little anticlimactic to be informed of Yoyo's Books survival via text, but that was what happened when one hermited.
Shelia had not left the house except to do groceries. She'd spent her time working on gigs, and when she didn't have any more, she turned to TV to fill her time.

She didn't let herself know that she was hiding, because then she'd have to figure out what she was hiding from, and really, who wanted to bother with that?

She looked over her messages once again. She was just past the acceptable window of time to reply back: therefore, she further avoided responding to them. But one message—an email, specifically—did loom large in her head.

Subject: Job Offer

Hi Shelia,

We are excited to formally offer you a designer role at Press Pros. Start dates are flexible, but it would work well for us to have you start on the 12th. Please see the attached document for salary and benefits information. Let me know if you have any questions or would like to discuss the offer in more detail. We would be delighted to welcome you to the team.

Sally Dunforth
HR of Press Pros Inc.

Technically Shelia should have felt happy at the prospect of being gainfully employed once again. *I mean, I did feel happy when I first read it.* But soon afterwards the reality of returning to the nine-to-five world struck her. If she had felt absolutely miserable or absolutely joyed about it, the decision might've been easier, but as such, she felt neither.

So she avoided the email as well. But the fact that the email had a shorter window of acceptable response time was making her anxious.

She switched on the television. Lorraine, a vengeful mama, was in the middle of roasting her daughter about her new boyfriend choice when Shelia's buzzer rang through her phone.

"Hey kid, will ya open up?" Yoyo said.

"Yoyo?" Shelia said, blinking. She'd never considered Yoyo physically existing outside of the bookstore. "Ummm… sure, come on up. Room 207."

"So, this is your place, eh?" Yoyo said, once inside.

"Yep."

Yoyo nodded, saying, "Monica said it would be nice but 'weirdly clean'. It's a little messy in here, kid. But I guess you weren't expecting me, eh."

Shelia shrugged. Her place *would* usually be clean, surprise guests or not. This time she hadn't noticed the buildup of dishes, clothes, packaging, and such.

Alright. Yoyo is here. Weird. Shelia wondered what to do about this. She stared blankly at Yoyo and Yoyo looked back at her, amused.

Slowly her hosting instincts kicked in, and she went for the tea. Yoyo followed her into the kitchen.

"Uh… Do you want lemon, green, or earl grey?"

"Whatever you're havin'," Yoyo said, taking a seat at her small kitchen table.

Shelia set the two cups down when they were ready and took a seat herself. "Congrats on the fundraiser being successful, Yoyo. It's really great news."

"What are ya talkin' about, congrats? The whole damn thing wouldn'ta happened without ya! Which is why we were waitin' for you to come by after the count. But you never showed up, did ya eh?"

Shelia didn't respond immediately, instead blowing on her tea. The steam tickled her nose. "No," she said, still looking into her tea. "So," she said, "you've come to dispense life advice to me, then?"

"Only if you want to, kid," Yoyo said kindly. "We can also just be friends havin' tea." She raised her cup.

Uncertainly, Shelia raised her cup as well. "So… how do you feel about Yoyo's not being dead?"

"I feel great. It's reinvigorating, all the possibilities we got, for the future. How do *you* feel?"

"I… feel the same way. I'm excited to expand upon the coding class." She sipped her tea.

Yoyo sipped her tea.

Staring into the abyss of her teacup, she said, "To be honest… the coding class feels like the only meaningful thing I'm doing."

"Really. What happened to that old lady you're visiting, eh? She die?"

"Um," Shelia said, taking a bigger sip of tea than she'd intended, "Yes."

Yoyo nodded thoughtfully. "How're ya feelin'?"

Shelia shrugged. "I mean, I don't know… it's sad but kind of inevitable… I did like visiting her, she could be sweet… I mean…" She tapped her fingers. "I think the dying itself wasn't half as bad as the fact that she… she oozed misery. I thought at that age you would come to peace with things. But Miss Moon was so sad, and afraid. Afraid to let go even until the very end."

"I see," is all Yoyo said.

The ensuing silence invited Shelia to continue, "I feel kind of haunted by it. I don't know why, I mean, I shouldn't be, right?"

Yoyo snorted. "You're havin' a feelin', and on top of that you're policin' the fact that you're feelin' things?"

"Don't judge me for my ineffective emotional processing," Shelia mumbled.

Yoyo didn't say anything, studying Shelia closely instead. Smiling, she took both of Shelia's hands.

"Listen, kid," she said, while Shelia felt confused about the gesture, "Miss Moon was not fortunate enough t' find her spirit in this lifetime. But you won't have the same fate as her. You have a will to *live*." She punctuated the last word by jabbing a finger on Shelia's heart.

"Ow," Shelia said off-handedly, surprised by the stinging in her eyes. Blinking hard, she asked, "How do you know, Yoyo?"

"You won't let yourself. And we won't let yourself," Yoyo said simply.

Shelia nodded, allowing the tears to fall.

"So, you're going to take that web design job?" Olivia asked, blowing the steam off of her phō.

"Well. I did and I didn't," Shelia said, pinching noodles between her chopsticks. "I had a bit of anxiety about whether or not to take it. On one hand, Press Pros seemed like it was a great company. But on the other, I was scared I would end up miserable again. But then again I thought, surely not all nine-to-five equals doom, and if it didn't work out, I could always change," she said. "I went back and forth like this, for a while. I realized at the heart of it—I'm not passionate about corporations, I'm passionate about the work itself. I'm more well-suited to freelancing than to working for companies. I mean, I really like my freelancing lifestyle! There's a different kind of stress to it, but I love the freedom. I have more time to do more things, like expand the Coding 101 seshes, and hang out with friends, and read more books. And recently I've picked up more clients than ever before—I'm finally happy with how my bank balance is going since I've quit. And I really think I can maintain that momentum."

"So I thought about it, and I told Press Pros that I'm not really an office type. But that I could work for them on a freelancing basis. They agreed, and decided to put me on retainer."

"Wow, Shelia," Olivia said, approving. "Look at you! I'm impressed by your moxie, as always."

Shelia smiled, appreciating Olivia's praise. "Honestly, though," she said, "I'm still scared. What if I can't manage? What if despite all of my efforts, I still fall flat on my face? What if I still end up miserable?"

"Listen, Shelia," Olivia said, "you are a master of reinvention. From what you've told me—you left a long-term partner and job in Waterloo, and started all over here. Then you made the ballsy—"

"—some would say stupid—"

"—move to quit your job," Olivia continued, smiling. "You already started your own hustle. You already built up all these new connections with people and created a space for them to learn. Shelia, you've exercised your *choice*. That will always be there for you. And we will be there for you. Accountability buddies, carving out a life, yeah?"

Shelia took a minute to absorb the words, looking silently at Olivia. She noted the parallels between what Olivia was saying and what Yoyo had told her. "Yeah," she said finally.

"You know you've inspired me, right?" Olivia said, after swallowing down phō.

"Really?" Shelia asked, chopsticks mid-air.

"This kind of segues into my own big news, but I've accepted a HR position at a new company."

"Yeah?" Shelia said. "Which?"

Olivia hesitated. "I think that you, particularly, will laugh at me if I tell you," she said.

"Okay, I promise I won't. Tell me!"

"A health and wellness company," Olivia said cautiously. "Zen Boogie."

"Zen Boogie, hey?" Shelia laughed. "I know that company."

"Hey, you promised!"

"I'm not laughing at you, Olivia," Shelia said. "I'm laughing because it's perfect for you. It seems like your dream job." Olivia smiled, eyes gleaming. She raised her tea cup. "To meaningful work," she said.

"To a meaningful life," Shelia said, clinking her glass of water with Olivia's tea.

The fields were lush and green, pulsating as the wind rolled through. Birds, perched on an oak, chirped serenely.

"WAKE THE FUCK UP," boomed the narrator, the scene switching to a frazzled-looking employee.

Reaching for more popcorn, Shelia glanced at the people seated around her, all gathered to watch the movie version of 'A Practical Guide to Life': Jeremiah, Monica, Olivia, Justin, Elizabeth, Dipon, and Yoyo. *In a weird way, none of this would have happened without that damn book.* Yoyo caught her eye and Shelia knew she was thinking of the weird full circle nature of it all, too.

Acknowledgements

The birth of this book was winding and twisting, and involved many characters throughout its formation.

First I would like to acknowledge everyone from the GYSD (Get Yo Shit Done) team — as I often say, those first couple of meets allowed space for a random little excerpt to eventually become a novel. Particularly from the GYSD team I would like to thank Fraser for his steady involvement at the beginning of GYSD, Jenna for infusing and transforming GYSD with her human-tea-cup essence, and lastly, Alessandra—for sticking with the formation of this book since day one, always diligently willing to give some feedback on whatever number draft I was on, and generally being a major support. Thanks as well to Liz, Loren, Brandon, and Kenneth for their valuable feedback on the book.

I would like to thank David Delafield for his copyediting.

I would also like to thank Taz Bouchier for her generous and crucial insights on how to approach the respectful representation of Indigenous culture, and acknowledge wherearethechildren.ca as a critical research resource. I would also like to acknowledge the land I'm living on, to which I'm deeply connected (Treaty 6 Territory), and the peoples who have traditionally gathered and resided here, and who continue to do so.

Shout-out to my parents for generally giving birth to me and raising me. You know who you are!

Lastly, I would like to thank you, the reader, for interacting with this chance piece of my brain, and giving it a unique life as you do. Hope you enjoyed it.

Also available by Tasmia Nishat: No Man's Land, a free short story

In the aftermath of an underwhelming break-up, Rashida receives a wedding invitation from an old ex. (No, not the one that she most recently broke up with–another ex.) Finally, it's a chance to prove how freaking awesome she is doing without her ex, thankyouverymuch.
Or is it her chance to be a hot mess at her ex's wedding?
Old friends and new friends help her through one trying wedding, in an all-night adventure.

Leave a Review

Reviews are invaluable for indie authors to get the word out about their work! If you liked *Some Effing Advice*, do consider leaving a review.

About the Author

Tasmia Nishat is a person who is interested in basically everything. Her interests include science, social justice, history, animation… It's a good thing that she writes good and can implement all these damn interests into her writing. Otherwise she would be doomed to float in the ether, flitting from interest to interest. *Some Effing Advice* is her first full-length work.

You can stay up-to-date with her writings by following her on Facebook, or checking out tasmianishat.com.

Copyright Notice

www.ingramcontent.com/pod-product-compliance
Lightning Source LLC
Chambersburg PA
CBHW050409260626
47156CB00003B/938